Hannah tossed cu

settled beside him,

a rug, an open fire, a contented dog and pups—and this man—where else would she want to be?

"Tit for tat," she said blithely. "You want to know why an Irish midwife is stuck on Camel Island with no one to call to say I won't be home tonight? Then I want to know why a neurosurgeon with the skills you have is hunkered down on Camel Island with—as far as I know—no one even worrying that there's a cyclone bearing down on you. Plus, you have a very interesting scar on your face. I need your story. So here goes, Dr. O'Connor. I'll tell you mine and you'll tell me yours."

Dear Reader,

I've always had a fascination with islands—the wilder, the more windswept, the better. My fantasy is to be a lighthouse keeper. How cool would that be?

Answer, very cool, but possibly not very comfortable—and ever so slightly isolated.

My answer has been to live on the tip of a peninsula, in my imagination an island, but with an opt-out spit connecting me to supermarkets, cinemas and good coffee.

But my fantasy remains, and thus I give you Josh, a damaged doctor whose island protects his wounded heart. Until Hannah—a gorgeous midwife with baggage, babies and puppies—arrives, building her own bridge to the man's heart.

I had a whole lot of fun writing Josh and Hannah's story. Thus I give you the island of my dreams, but with opt-outs included. Sometimes we need an island. Sometimes we need life.

Marion Lennox

PREGNANT MIDWIFE ON HIS DOORSTEP

MARION LENNOX

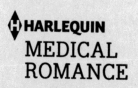

HARLEQUIN®
MEDICAL ROMANCE™

Recycling programs
for this product may
not exist in your area.

ISBN-13: 978-1-335-14955-8

Pregnant Midwife on His Doorstep

Copyright © 2020 by Marion Lennox

This edition published by arrangement with Harlequin Books S.A.

For questions and comments about the quality of this book,
please contact us at CustomerService@Harlequin.com.

Harlequin Enterprises ULC
22 Adelaide St. West, 40th Floor
Toronto, Ontario M5H 4E3, Canada
www.Harlequin.com

Printed in U.S.A.

Marion Lennox has written over one hundred romance novels and is published in over one hundred countries and thirty languages. Her international awards include the prestigious RITA® Award (twice!) and the *RT Book Reviews* Career Achievement Award for "a body of work which makes us laugh and teaches us about love." Marion adores her family, her kayak, her dog and lying on the beach with a book someone else has written. Heaven!

Books by Marion Lennox

Harlequin Medical Romance

Bondi Bay Heroes
Finding His Wife, Finding a Son

Falling for Her Wounded Hero
Reunited with Her Surgeon Prince
The Baby They Longed For
Second Chance with Her Island Doc
Rescued by the Single Dad Doc

Harlequin Romance

Stranded with the Secret Billionaire
The Billionaire's Christmas Baby
English Lord on Her Doorstep
Cinderella and the Billionaire

Visit the Author Profile page
at Harlequin.com for more titles.

With thanks to the wonderful Kate Hicks, who
delivered Maisie's puppies with skill
and friendship.

CHAPTER ONE

HIS NEIGHBOUR MUST be evacuating her dog—but this late?

Dr Josh O'Connor had been watching the forecast for the last twenty-four hours. Cyclone Alma was supposed to stay well north of Camel Island, but the weather was building to extreme. When the radio broadcaster had said, 'An unpredicted change has the eye of the storm veering south,' Josh had started to have serious qualms. Should he leave?

But he'd looked through his sturdy double-glazed windows and seen the heaving sea, he'd thought of the rickety bridge across to the mainland and he'd decided it'd be safer to hunker down. His house was new, long, low, solid and set on the lee side of the island. Heavy shutters provided protection. He had plenty of provisions. The storm might cut him off from the mainland for a few days but he'd be fine.

But what about the others? He barely knew the residents of the only two other houses on this remote island, but he knew enough to worry. By mid-afternoon, with the change in weather prediction, he'd tried to contact them.

The house on the far side of the island was occupied by a couple of artists and their kids, and his phone call had made him feel like he was overreacting. 'We'll be right, mate,' Mick Forde had told him. 'Skye and me have seen storms like this before. It'll give us something to paint. We're staying.' Josh had thought of their ramshackle cottage with misgivings but there was nothing he could do in the face of their intransigence.

The only other house was on his side of the island, owned by the very elderly Moira Byrne. She was a loner. When Josh had first arrived and introduced himself, she'd been curt to the point of rudeness.

'If you think we're going to play happy neighbours think again. I bought this place because of its isolation and that's the way I like it. Keep out of my way and I'll keep out of yours.'

He had, though her frailty and solitude had him concerned. Once a week she drove her ancient white sedan across the bridge, presumably heading to the town on the mainland for supplies. Occasionally a little red car arrived and someone stayed for a few hours, but whoever it was kept to themselves as well. The driver of the red car seemed to be Miss Byrne's only personal contact, but Josh was the last person to want to encroach on her solitude.

But this afternoon he'd been uneasy enough to intrude. Her phone had rung out so he'd battled his way over there. He'd heard a dog whining inside but there'd been no other response to repeated knocking. The house and garage were locked, curtained, shuttered.

He'd stood on her doorstep in the rising wind and decided she must have headed to the mainland because of the storm. He wished he could see inside the garage to confirm her car wasn't there, but he imagined her staying in a mainland motel overnight, where a dog wouldn't be welcome. She must have locked her dog inside to be safe.

There was a dog flap set in the back door. The dog could come outside if it wanted to, but it obviously wasn't interested enough in Josh's knocking or calling to investigate. Fair enough, Josh decided, thinking of his own dog's fear of storms. He'd check again in the morning but he could do no more. He'd headed home, hunkered down in his office and immersed himself in his work.

Technology's role in medicine had always fascinated him, and the use of external robotic skeletons in the hope of restoring function to patients with spinal damage had become his passion. After his own accident it had been easy enough to leave hands-on testing to his staff. Retreating to the complexities of techno-science, he led his team from the seclusion of his office. He drove to the city when he was most needed. He attended overseas conferences, but otherwise he worked alone.

The project he was working on was vital and enthralling, but it wasn't enough to block out the storm. Dudley—the misbegotten mutt he'd been landed with when he'd bought this place—didn't help. He was cowering under Jock's office chair in what Josh imagined was the doggy equivalent of the foetal position, and his whimpers were getting louder.

'It's okay, boy,' he told him, but Dudley looked at him as if he was a sandwich short of a picnic and went back to whimpering.

By dusk the phone lines were out and his generator had cut in to augment battery storage from his solar power. This place was designed for self-sufficiency. Josh had power for refrigeration and lights, a slow combustion stove providing central heating and hot water, plus enough driftwood to keep both the stove and the open fire in the living room lit for months. He had a pantry and freezer full of supplies. His very expensive satellite dish was still giving him connectivity to the outside world if he needed it. Dudley might be worried, but he wasn't.

'Let's cook some dinner,' he told him.

Dudley was still looking at him as if he was

nuts. He was under Josh's chair and he was staying there.

'Wuss,' Josh told him, but got down on his hands and knees and started scratching Dudley's ears. Dudley just whimpered.

Okay, he'd bring out the big guns—Dudley's favourite thing in the whole world. Josh lay on his back, patted his chest and waited.

His strategy worked. The scrawny kelpie gave a final worried whine, but this was a ruse Josh had used since he'd found the half-starved, flea-ridden mutt when he'd moved here. The anxiety-ridden dog could never resist. Now he inched forward from under the chair, then slithered cautiously up onto Josh's chest. Josh rubbed Dudley's spine in the way dogs the world over loved, and hugged him tight.

Which worked both ways. Josh might be self-reliant, he conceded, but the storm was a big one and he wasn't completely impervious to it. A hug from a dog was okay.

'We're both wusses,' he told Dudley, and Dudley signified his solidarity with a lick from throat to chin.

Bleah.

'Dinner,' Josh said, grinning as he wiped away spit. Dudley heaved a resigned sigh that said he ought to worry more about the storm but maybe he'd put dinner first. Josh hugged him again, then headed to the kitchen, with Dudley slinking cautiously after him. He filled Dudley's bowl with kibble, then decided to check outside. He'd closed the shutters this afternoon, making it impossible to see through the windows, but now he cautiously opened the back door.

Josh's house, made of stone and hunkered among a couple of rocky outcrops, still seemed solidly safe, but outside seemed just plain scary. The wind was screaming. Debris was blasting against the walls. Josh's instinct was to close the door fast—but then he paused. There were car lights heading along the track from Moira's house, down toward the bridge.

Had Moira had second thoughts and come back for her dog? He hadn't seen her return, but then his windows had been shuttered. She must have come back, collected her dog and decided to retreat again.

Across the bridge? His vague worries about his elderly neighbour suddenly coalesced into fear.

He'd had qualms about the bridge when he'd bought this place, but a call to the local council had reassured him. An unmanned but essential lighthouse on the far side of the island meant the bridge always had to stay connected. Council had budgeted for a rebuild in the next financial year.

But this wasn't the next financial year, and no one had predicted a cyclone this far south. There'd be waves smashing against the pilings, and Josh had seen the ancient timbers creak and sway in the last storm. Which hadn't been as bad as this.

Now he was watching the car lights head toward it, and he found he'd forgotten to breathe.

He was overreacting, he told himself. The bridge had withstood weather for decades and it'd take the car less than a minute to cross.

For a moment a car's headlights illuminated the timbers as the car slowed. Moira had obviously paused to assess the situation.

The decision was made. The headlights inched forward, onto the bridge itself.

And then lurched violently and disappeared.

'*Hell.*'

And that was the least of the swear words he uttered as he hauled on his boots and headed through the internal door to the garage. He hit the remote on the doors, the wind blasted in—and seconds later he was out in the teeth of the storm.

At least his truck was sturdy. He'd bought it because it was tough, because he valued the ease of driving along the rough tracks to the island's isolated beaches. Now he valued its sheer weight.

He thought of Moira's tiny sedan. No one should be driving in these conditions, and the swerve of those lights… They'd pointed upwards and then disappeared.

He was gunning down the track like a madman. If the bridge had gone… If Moira's car had crashed into the sea…

There'd be nothing he could do. He knew it even before he reached the bridge. The channel across to the mainland was deep and fast flowing. This side of the island was in the lee of the storm but even so, the waves would be crashing through with force. A tiny car, submerged…

He needed help.

He didn't have it.

The phone lines and cell-phone connectivity had failed hours ago. With self-sufficiency in mind—and because he relied on video conferencing for his work—Josh had paid the horrendous price for satellite connection, but anyone in that water would be dead long before outside assistance could arrive.

He reached the bridge—or what was left of it. His headlights lit the scene and he saw a storm-washed wreck.

The bridge had crashed, its timbers now a jumbled mass, tilted sideways into the sea, already separating and being washed away.

A car was in that jumble.

It was still on this side, though, in the water but only just. The bridge must have crumbled almost as soon as it was fully on its timbers.

And it wasn't Moira's car. Moira's car was white. This was a tiny, indeterminate red thing. The car he'd seen occasionally visit.

And whoever was in it was in dire trouble. Its bonnet was almost submerged. Timbers were all around it and waves were thumping the wood. The car was slewing sideways...

He was out of his truck before he knew it, plunging down the bank, around the mass of loose planking, leaving his headlights playing the scene.

A massive plank was wedged against the driver's door. It was being shoved by more timbers. The car was being pushed further in.

He could see a face at the driver's window. A woman's face, framed by a mass of copper-red curls. A mask of terror.

He couldn't get to her.

He stopped for a millisecond, giving himself time to evaluate. Training kicked in. From the moment he'd enrolled in medical school, procedure had been drilled in, over and over. No matter what the emergency, assess the whole situation before acting.

This must be the world record for speed assessment, but it was worthwhile. The waves were hammering the plank against the car so strongly it'd be useless to try to reach the driver's door and attempt to pull it away. He couldn't do it. But the plank was angled, and the biggest force of the waves would be at the front of the car, where the water was deepest.

It felt counterintuitive but he backed away, further up the bank from the driver's door, to the far end of the plank holding the door.

Could he? He had no choice. He got behind the end of the plank, trying to brace himself against the water, against the blasting wind. He pushed with all his might.

The force of the water at the other end was now his friend. He could feel the timber tremble, then shift...

And suddenly move. The plank was suddenly caught by the current, tumbling out to midstream to be tossed away to the sea.

That left the little car without the plank's protection from the waves, but at least it wasn't wedging the door closed.

He surged in and grabbed the door handle. The woman inside was obviously pushing. He pulled—no, he hauled. The water was holding it shut, but with their combined strength the door finally opened. He shoved it back against the water's force, made his body a wedge to stop it slamming shut again and reached in.

The woman was struggling. She was youngish. Soaked. Small but bulky. Terrified.

He grabbed her, hauled her out to him, steadied her.

'Is there anyone else in the car?' He was yelling but the wind was tossing his words to oblivion. He put his mouth hard against her ear. 'Is Moira in there?'

'No. But her dog's in there.' Her yell was fear-filled, loud enough to be heard. 'On the back seat.'

'No one else. Sure?'

'Just the dog.' She was pushing against him, struggling to reach the back door handle.

His first instinct was to fight her, to simply drag her up the bank and get her safe, but she'd already grabbed the handle. If they were hit by another of the timbers…

But they had this moment. There was a chance…

He had his arm around her, and her bulky midriff helped, making their combined bodies a barrier against the water's force.

'Pull,' he yelled, and she tugged. The door swung wide and the surging water held it open.

But with both doors open, the car was starting to move.

'She's on the seat,' the woman screamed, but Josh's priorities had suddenly changed. As he'd held her he'd realised her midriff wasn't the squishy waist of plumpness. It was the firm mound of pregnancy.

She was caught between two doors.

Triage kicked in. He hauled her away from the car, to shore and then up the bank, ignoring fierce, fiery protests. 'Get yourself safe,' he yelled. 'Are you nuts? Your baby… Get into my truck!'

'The dog…'

'Now!' he yelled, and she relented, allowing herself to be shoved to safety. But on the bank, instead of heading to the truck, she turned back to him with anguish.

'The dog…' she screamed. 'Maisie… Please…'

He looked back, torn. The car's bonnet was starting to swerve downstream. He had milliseconds.

He lunged back into the water, reaching the car again, groping into the back seat, knowing his chances were tiny.

His hands met a great lump of wet fur. Limp. Injured?

The car shuddered and moved.

Somehow he had her, by collar, by scruff. She came free with a rush, and he staggered and almost fell.

Another wave crashed into his legs. He went down to his waist in the water, but held position, held dog.

The car shifted more, slewing sideways. His arms were full of dog. He was struggling to find his feet.

And then the woman was back, staggering into the wash, grabbing his arm. 'Let me help.'

'Get back.'

'No. Move!'

She didn't release his arm. She was hauling him toward the bank and her extra force helped.

Somehow he was on his feet. She was holding him, tugging.

And then they were staggering out of the water, surging upwards, not stopping until they were up the bank, not stopping until they collapsed in a sodden heap against his truck, safe from the wind.

As if on cue, there was a crash of timbers. In the beam of his headlights they watched another plank smash against the car.

The car rolled and tumbled and disappeared in the wash of white water.

And was gone.

For a moment neither of them spoke. Josh was having trouble breathing. Maybe he'd forgotten how. He sat slumped against the truck, his arms full of dog, feeling…gutted.

Unbidden, the thought came back of another accident, three years back. Of sitting just like this, waiting for the ambulance. Of hopelessness. Of despair.

'Thank you.'

The woman's voice cut across his thoughts, dragging him out of his nightmare. He thought of her trapped in the car as the water rose. Of her terror. He could feel the blackness…

Get over yourself, he told himself fiercely. This is a happy ending. Nothing like last time.

It was almost still in the lee provided by the

truck, though maybe that was just comparative. It was quiet compared to the blast of wind in the open. Just standing was hard. How had they managed to do what they'd done?

'What the hell were you doing, trying to cross the bridge?' he snapped. Emotions were coalescing into a wave of anger. He saw her flinch, and hauled back himself.

'Sorry. We're safe. Explain later. Where's Moira?' She'd come from Moira's house. He'd expected Moira to be in the car. Why else would she be here but to take Moira to safety? But if Moira had already left… Had Moira sent her to fetch her dog?

'Moira's dead.' Her voice was flat, no inflection, leaving no doubts. Shocking.

'What the…?'

But if he was shocked, soaked, bruised, how much more so was this woman? The headlights weren't much use this far around the car but there was enough light for an impression. The woman was…youngish? She had coppery red hair, curls dripping to her shoulders. Not tall. Not plump either, as he'd first thought. She was wearing pants and a loose top, which was now clinging wetly. She looked very pregnant.

He needed to bundle her back to the house and get her warm. There was also the issue of a limp dog. Injured?

But triage… Moira. Dead?

'Explain,' he said, curtly. If Moira really was dead there was nothing he could do, but he'd heard enough anguished screaming from relatives during his medical career... 'He's dead, Doctor...' to know the diagnosis wasn't always right.

But she must have heard his doubt because it was addressed straight away.

'I'm a nurse,' the woman managed, and he heard the strong lilt of an Irish accent. 'I'm a midwife but I know death when I see it. Moira's my great-aunt. She's a loner, and she hates me coming, but she has a heart condition so I visit when I can, like it or not. When I heard the forecast I rang to ask her to evacuate. She told me where to go. Then this afternoon she rang me back, in a state. She sounded terrified, gaspy. She wasn't feeling well and asked if I could come. I suggested an ambulance but she snapped my head off. So I came. She...she was sitting by the kitchen fire, the dog at her feet. Almost peaceful. It took me two hours to get here but by the look of things I suspect she'd been dead for almost that long.'

'I'm so sorry.' It seemed appallingly inadequate.

'I hardly knew her.' Her voice was almost a whisper. 'But she was all the family I had.'

He thought suddenly of his dog, of fear and of the need for the contact of another living thing.

There was so much bleakness in this woman's voice.

Triage. Sympathy would have to come later.

He rose and heaved the dog into the back seat. For the life of him he couldn't see what was wrong with her. She was a golden Labrador, fat, heavy, limp. She raised her head a little as he moved her, her huge brown eyes meeting his. Had she been struck by timbers? It didn't make sense, but what did make sense was getting them all out of this weather.

With the dog in the back seat he half lifted the woman to her feet and helped her into the passenger seat. Then he headed for the driver's side, which was no mean feat when that was the weather side.

The wind was still rising. If it got any stronger… He blocked the thought as he headed home. Home, with its remote-control garage doors, with its heat, with its safety.

'Where are we going?' the woman managed.

'To my place. The house you can see from Moira's.'

'But it's empty!' She said it almost as an accusation. 'Moira has your phone number on the fridge. I told her to ring you, but she said she couldn't. When I got here I looked across and there wasn't a light on. You think I would have tried to cross the bridge if I'd known I could get help there?' Her teeth were chattering so hard she could hardly get the words out, but indignation came through, loud and strong.

'I'm very sorry,' he said and he meant it. 'I shuttered the place down at lunchtime. I also tried to check on Moira but no one answered my knock. That's Moira through and through, though. I should have left a light on.'

'It might have been helpful.'

'It might.' He hesitated. 'You didn't think to stay at Moira's until the morning?'

'She's dead.'

'I get that, but—'

'But I didn't want to stay with my dead great-aunt.' Her indignation was still there. 'It felt like I had to let someone know, and I didn't know the bridge was going to crash. And the forecast says it'll get worse before it gets better. And then there's Maisie...'

'Maisie?'

'The dog. She's in trouble.' She glanced into the darkness of the back seat and indignation faded. 'I... Moira says...said...you're a doctor. Do you know anything about delivering puppies?'

'Delivering puppies...'

'Obstructed labour,' she said briefly, and her voice faltered, shock and stress flooding back. 'I'm sorry,' she said after a moment. 'I'm not... at my best. And I'm a midwife but I know nothing about labour in dogs. I could feel contractions half an hour ago, but they were getting weaker and so was she. The phone connection seems to be dead so I couldn't phone a vet. I couldn't get onto the internet to find out what I might be able to do and she's going to die and she's a lovely dog. And Moira's dead, which makes me feel sick to my stomach. And I'm freezing and I'm eight months pregnant and I'm scared. I *was* terrified. Thanks to you, I'm not any more but I'm still scared.' She took a deep breath, fighting against hysteria, and decided on indignation instead. 'And you should have put your outside light on.'

'I'm very sorry,' he said again.

'Thank you.' She took another breath and he could almost hear her gritting her teeth. 'If I were a heroine in a romance novel I'd have disintegrated into hysterics by now and left this whole mess to a knight on a white charger. But I needed him two hours ago. Now I'm over it. I don't know you from Adam but you've done all right so far, and I'm grateful. You're all I have in the knight on a white charger department, so please keep right on rescuing. Maisie's depending on you. I'm depending on you. You're all we have.'

And she put her face in her hands, gave one fierce sob and subsided.

CHAPTER TWO

SHE DIDN'T DISSOLVE into hysterics. She allowed herself that one, single sob and then she hauled herself together.

Somehow.

At least she hadn't been swept out to sea. How many times had she struggled for silver linings over the last few months? She was fighting for one now. Not being swept out to sea had to be close.

Oh, but she was cold.

But she was safe. This truck was built for toughness rather than style, but its engine sounded reassuringly powerful and it beavered its way along the track as if the storm wasn't trying its best to shove it backwards.

And the man beside her…

He looked as tough as his truck, she thought.

He was tall and broad and the hands on the steering wheel looked weathered, large, capable. His mouth was set in a grim line and his deep eyes were focused fiercely on the track ahead.

There seemed to be a scar running across his forehead, around his left eye to the base of his ear. It added to the aura of toughness. The impression she had was of strength, competence and certainty.

His ancient sweater was soaked and streaming water. His deep black hair was plastered across his forehead but the soaking just seemed to add to his aura of strength.

A knight on a white charger? Maybe not, but give her a hero with a serviceable truck any day. The thought made her hiccup on something between a laugh and a sob and he glanced at her sharply before returning his attention to the track.

'Don't you dare.'

'What?'

'Swoon or have hysterics.'

She almost managed a smile. 'Sorry. I didn't mean it.' Her teeth were chattering so hard it was almost impossible to speak but she forced herself to go on. 'If the books I've read are any indication of the remedies for either, isn't it a bucket of cold water? I've just copped an ocean.'

She saw his grim mouth relax a little. Half a smile?

She could see a light ahead—he must have finally put an outside light on. The sight was infinitely reassuring.

She needed this man's help. She needed to make herself sound sensible.

'I'm Hannah Byrne,' she told him. 'I'm a midwife, working at North Queensland Regional Hospital, and if the sticky note on Moira's fridge is to believed, you're Josh O'Connor. A doctor. Doctor of medicine?'

'Yes,' he said curtly. 'I insisted Moira keep my details. It would have been a sight more useful if she'd phoned me rather than a niece two hours' drive away. Two hours ago the lines were open. I could have been there in five minutes.'

'It would have nearly killed her to phone even me,' she said, and faltered. 'I guess…it did kill her.'

'Her stubbornness killed her,' he said bluntly. 'She knew I was home. If she managed to ring you she could have rung me.'

'Maybe dying at home's what she wanted anyway,' Hannah said softly. 'She would have hated hospital. All those people… She can't…couldn't stand people. I think she only rang me because she was frightened about Maisie. She was old and she was ill. I can't… I can't grieve.'

'You *are* grieving,' he said matter-of-factly, and she closed her eyes.

'I guess…for what could have been.' She hauled herself together again. 'But today… She obviously didn't feel well enough to drive Maisie to the vet, but I suspect it would have killed her to contact you. A stranger. A man…'

Her voice trailed off as she thought of the old

woman as she'd last seen her, slumped by the fire-side in death, her hand trailing down to touch her dog by her side.

But then they were at the house. Josh flicked the remote and the garage door slipped up seam-lessly. The inside light went on automatically and Hannah blinked in the shock of unexpected light.

'You have power.'

'Solar power augmented by batteries and a gen-erator.'

'Oh, my.' She took a deep breath. 'And phone?'

'Normal coverage seems to have been cut but I have a satellite.'

'A satellite phone? You can call for help?'

'I doubt help would be forthcoming,' he said, driving into the garage. 'Not in this storm. The latest forecast is for the cyclone's eye to pass within a hundred kilometres. This is going to get worse before it gets better.'

But as the garage door slid quietly down be-hind them the noise from the wind cut off. Just like that.

She was sitting in a silent, well-lit garage. With no storm.

Safe.

Maisie. She turned to look into the back seat. The big dog was still with them. She was looking at her with those huge eyes. Dependent.

Josh was right, though. There was no way they could call for evacuation for a dog.

Or for a great-aunt who'd died from natural causes.

She'd been shaking before but suddenly, weirdly, the shakes grew worse. Shock, fear, worry, and reaction from everything that had gone before was suddenly overwhelming. Her body seemed a trembling mess. She put her hands on either side of the seat and held on, trying to ground herself, trying to haul herself together.

But then Josh was around her side of the truck, and before she knew what he was about he'd lifted her out bodily.

'What...?' Her voice came out as an unidentifiable squeak. 'Put me down. I'm okay.'

'You're not okay,' he said, striding with her across the garage. Somehow he edged the door open, carrying into the house, lowering her a little to brush light switches on as he went.

She had a first impression of solidity, of stone floors, massive beams, of comfort. They entered the living room and she saw a fire in the hearth blazing with heat. She saw two great settees, club style, squishy, and a massive crimson rug.

A lanky, brown and black kelpie-like dog had been lying by the fire. He launched himself toward them, his skinny tail spinning like a gyrocopter. 'Back,' Josh ordered, and the spinning tail was instantly tucked between his legs. The dog cast Josh a look of deep reproach and retired back to the fire.

But Josh didn't pause. He was through the living room and out the other side, down the passage.

She felt warmth as they went. Central heating? Gorgeous.

Josh was pushing another door open. A bathroom. A wide, open shower. A bath.

A bath!

'A bath will be safer than a shower,' Josh suggested. Before she could respond he lowered her onto a stool and hit the taps. A gush of water streamed out, creating glorious steam. 'Otherwise I'll have to hold you up in the shower.' But then the impetus stopped. He knelt beside her and gripped her hands, his dark eyes meeting hers in concern. Professional concern? 'Hannah, tell me. Are you hurt in any way? Did you get hit when the car was swept down?'

Suddenly he'd turned into a doctor. Up until now he'd been a rescuer, a stranger with strength when she'd needed it. Now there was professional incisiveness.

'I… No.'

'Did you have your seat belt on?'

'Yes, but…'

'Can you feel your baby? Any movements?'

'I think so.' She faltered. Her hand went to her swollen abdomen. 'In the truck… I felt her kick. I'm sure…'

'Would you let me check? If it's okay with you

I need to listen to make sure she's okay. I have a stethoscope.'

'You really are a doctor?'

'I am,' he told her. 'A neurosurgeon—not that that's any help now. But my med training included Babies for Beginners. Will you let me examine you?'

'I… Yes. Of course.'

'Can you pull that sweater off while I fetch my gear? Or can I help?'

'I can… I can do it.'

'Back in ten seconds,' he told her, and slipped out of the room.

She tugged off her soaked sweater. The relief as its soaked, heavy weight disappeared was indescribable. Then her bra… There was a qualm, but she made it short. *Sod it, he's a doctor,* she told herself. He'd have seen worse things come out of cheese. She looked at the bath, which was already a quarter full. Gently steaming.

Irresistible.

He was a doctor. She could play the patient.

She kicked off her sneakers and tugged away her saturated pants. She left on her knickers—he might be a doctor but a girl had some standards—and she couldn't wait a moment longer. She lowered herself into the heavenly, heavenly water.

He walked back in and she was in the bath.

Almost naked.

Steam was rising around her. Her damp, copper-red curls were dripping in tendrils to her shoulders. She was cupping the warm water to her face, and he could almost feel her relief as the heat made contact with her skin.

She was Irish. He'd heard it in her voice and he saw it now on her skin. Irish complexion, porcelain white, smooth, flawless. Her breasts were full, beautiful. Her figure—probably diminutive before—was gorgeously rounded with pregnancy. As her hands dropped from her face she looked up at him and he saw details for the first time. Green eyes, wide and clear. A generous mouth and firm chin. A snub nose and a smattering of freckles.

'Stuff modesty, this is irresistible,' she told him, and managed to smile. He could still hear the shake behind her voice but there was no doubting the courage behind the words.

This was a woman who'd driven for two hours in filthy weather to check on a great-aunt who didn't like her. A woman who'd risked her life to save a dog.

Who was looking up at him now, almost naked, beautiful...

Trusting.

Because he was a doctor, he told himself harshly. That was why she trusted him. It was amazing what a medical degree conferred.

'Can you help Maisie?' she faltered, and he

hauled his thoughts away from her—or a little away from her—and focused on priorities.

'She's still in the truck.'

'Josh…'

'If you're a nurse then you know the drill,' he said. 'People before animals.'

'I'm fine.'

'And your baby?' He hauled the stool up beside the bath and fitted his stethoscope to his ears.

She subsided. He was right. She had been wearing a seat belt and it would have tightened hard across her belly as the car had lurched downwards. She felt another flood of fear, this time almost overwhelming, but Josh already had his 'scope on her belly. listening intently.

And then smiling.

'You want to listen?' he said, and moved the earpieces to her.

She listened.

The warm water was still gushing into the bath. Any minute now her belly would be totally submerged. The warmth… The feel of Josh's hands as he fitted the 'scope into her ears… The *wush-wush* of her baby's strong, regular, wonderful, miraculous heartbeat…

She was suddenly stupidly, idiotically crying.

She didn't cry. She never cried. Not when Ryan had walked out on her. Not when her father had told her of the reception she'd get if she went home. Not once.

Now, though, the tears slipped down her face and she had no hope of stopping them. And then Josh was dipping a facecloth into the warm water and putting it into her hands, propelling it to her face. Asking gently, 'Where does is hurt?' and waiting with patience while she hauled herself together to say she was fine.

'You've been lucky, though I'm betting you'll ache in the morning. I can see bruises on your arms—that must have been from when you were trying to get out—and I'll bet you have others.' He had the stethoscope back and now he listened to *her* heart. 'Good,' he said. 'Mum and bub, hearts beating almost in sync. Lovely and strong.'

The relief was good. The relief was great.

'But Maisie,' she managed, because that's what her mad dash over the bridge had all been about.

'I'm going.' He motioned to the bars at the side of the bath. 'Use these if you need to get out.'

'Geriatric bars?' She almost had herself back together and was able to take in the bathroom. To say it was generous was the least of it. The shower was walk-in. The bath had innocuous silver rails running its length. The floor was lined with soft green rubber, unnoticeable unless you'd spent your career in hospitals and recognised hospital-grade non-slip surfaces.

'I live on my own and I'm not stupid,' Josh told her. 'They're not geriatric bars, they're sensible bars. If you knew how many injuries I've treated from people slipping in bathrooms... Use them, Hannah. Promise, or I need to stay here until you're out.'

'I'll use them.'

'Good girl.' He pulled fluffy white towels from a shelf running beneath the basin and hung them on what looked like a heated towel rail, and then motioned to a bathrobe hanging on the door.

'Use that if you need to get out before I return, but don't rush,' he told her. 'Don't let the water get any hotter than it is now.' He handed her a plastic jug from the same shelf. 'You might want to rinse your hair. Stay where you are until the shakes stop completely. I'll take care of Maisie.'

'Josh, this place...this equipment...you have everything.'

'I like to be prepared,' he told her, with the hint of a smile. 'Like your aunt, I value my independence and this place has been built to provide it.'

Then he stooped and touched her face, brushing the backs of his fingers gently across her cheek. It was a feather touch, no more. A touch of reassurance. 'You're safe now,' he said gently. 'You take care of you and your baby, and leave everything else to me.'

And he walked out.

She was alone. She was in Josh's care.

Involuntarily her fingers strayed to touch her cheek where his fingers had brushed.

There was no reason at all for her to put her

hand where his fingers had brushed…as if it had been a gift beyond measure.

No reason at all.

Triage.

Dog.

Himself.

He was soaking and despite the warmth of the house he was starting to shake. If he'd been alone he'd be in the shower, enjoying the same hot water that was doing so much good to Hannah. But Hannah's dog was in trouble and she'd almost lost her life saving it. The dog had to come first.

Or almost first. He wasn't stupid and he could hardly function when he was sodden and freezing. He ditched his clothes, towelled himself dry and grabbed more pants, a sweater and thick socks. Then he headed back out through the living room. Dudley rose to greet him. With obvious reproach.

'Sorry, mate.' He bent to give him a swift hug. Dudley had been a bundle of nerves when he'd found him and this wind wasn't doing his nerves any good now. But Josh had a sick, wet dog in the car and the fireside was the obvious place to bring her.

'Needs must,' he said apologetically, and carried Dudley's basket into the laundry. He gave him a chew bone and an extra hug, then firmly closed the door. He knew Dudley would shake again but he couldn't help it.

Hannah's dog… Moira's dog…was still where he'd left her. When he pulled open the truck door she raised her head to looked at him, huge brown eyes almost pleading. Then her eyes filled with panic. Her sides heaved. He laid a hand on her sodden fur and felt it ripple with a contraction, then lose strength. The panic faded and her head fell back, all strength lost.

Trouble.

A layman would be able to sense that this dog was in deep distress. Even the way she responded as he lifted her from the truck… He was a stranger, yet there was no hint of protest. Now the contraction was past, she was totally limp.

He carried her through to the living room and laid her in front of the fire. Then he grabbed an armload of towels from the laundry—which meant another apology to Dudley—and rubbed her. Her thick coat meant that getting her totally dry was impossible but he had to get her warm enough to prevent shock.

Or more shock.

As he towelled, her abdomen tightened again. Her tail was up, her rear distended.

The birth canal seemed to be slightly open but he could see no sign of a pup. In a human he could do a manual examination. In a dog?

Hannah had found her in trouble. She'd said

she was a midwife and she'd have done her own assessment. If things had been progressing normally, she wouldn't have made the mad dash over the bridge. Maisie must have been like this for at least an hour, probably a lot longer. Since before Moira had called Hannah?

He knew nothing about dogs.

Internet. Thank heaven for satellite phones. He fetched his laptop, did a fast search and found enough to realise how dire Maisie's situation was.

'What's happening?'

He hadn't noticed Hannah's arrival. She was in the doorway, wrapped in his big, fleecy bathrobe. Her wet curls were tied up in a towel, with wisps of red escaping. She was staring worriedly down at Maisie.

'It has to be obstructed labour,' he said briefly.

'Yeah.' She crossed and sank beside her dog, who whined a futile greeting and then went back to staring sightlessly at the pain within.

'I don't know what to do,' she told him. 'I tried to do an internal examination but there's no room. If there's a pup stuck it's still high in the birth canal. Too high to manoeuvre. Oh, Maisie…' Her voice broke.

'You love her?' It sounded harsh but he needed to know.

'No. Or maybe.' She shrugged. 'It's just… I've only been in Australia for a few months. Moira's my only relative here and she didn't want anything to do with me. But my Gran back home asked me to check on her, so I did, like it or not. Moira was never pleased to see me but even that first time Maisie was all joy to have a visitor. Every time I came Maisie's been greeting me like I was her new best friend. It sounds pathetic but she seems…more family than Moira was.'

He got it.

She did love this dog.

It made things more complicated.

'I need to phone a vet,' he told her.

'The phones don't work.'

'My satellite connection keeps mine working.'

That made her eyebrows hike. She sat back on her heels and stared at him, accusing. 'Really? Why didn't you give that number to Moira?'

'To ring someone on a satellite connection when normal coverage is out then you need a satellite phone yourself,' he said absently, still thinking of options. 'Moira only had a landline.' He frowned as she bent over the limp Maisie. Hannah herself was *very* pregnant. 'Hannah, your baby…you'd tell me if you were having contractions?'

'As if that'll happen,' she said, swiftly indignant. 'I have at least four weeks to go and any baby of mine has more sense than to come now.'

He smiled and moved on. 'Good. Can you keep rubbing Maisie? I want her as dry as possible. I'll call the vet from the kitchen.'

'Won't any vet be hunkered down with the cyclone?'

'I have research friends all over the world,' he told her. 'Including veterinarians. I'll choose somewhere where it's daylight and sunny. Keep her as warm as you can while I find us some help.'

The easiest option with a dog this far gone, with its mistress dead, was one he could handle. There'd been a seal wounded on the rocks only weeks before, far too badly injured to recover. He'd figured what to do and he had the drugs to do it. But Hannah's face, and her words—*'She seems more family'*—had had an impact. There'd been real distress.

She'd almost lost her life trying to save Maisie. The least he could do was try.

Tom Edmonton, Melbourne based, was involved in the same research Josh was doing, though he'd been working with dogs with spinal damage. He listened to Josh's story and then gave his considered opinion.

'Josh, that's real trouble.'

'Tell me something I don't know.'

'Equipment? Drugs?'

'I have some. Tell me what I need.'

'I can't,' Tom admitted. 'I haven't coped with a pregnant bitch for years. But we have working vets in this building. Claire Chapter's one of our senior partners. I'll see if she's available.'

'Tom, I need help fast. We're running out of time.'

'And if she dies? Given what you've told me, you know that's the likely option.'

'Just put me through to Claire and let me try.'

CHAPTER THREE

HANNAH SAT BY Josh's wonderful fire, soaking in the warmth, listening to the wind howling outside, savouring the sensation of feeling safe—and agonising over the dog beside her.

Why was her heart so gutted because a dog was dying?

When she'd walked into Moira's house and found her aunt dead she'd felt grief for a life filled with bitterness, but she'd felt no deep wrench of her own heart. But Maisie...

She remembered the first time she'd met the dog. She'd just arrived in Australia. After three years of travelling, she and Ryan had found jobs at North Queensland Regional Hospital. She had a local great-aunt. To an increasingly homesick Hannah, the prospect of visiting Moira had seemed a little piece of home.

It hadn't worked out that way. Firstly Ryan had refused to come with her—*'Didn't we leave Ireland to escape family?'*—and then Moira had shown resentment at the intrusion and nothing else. Only Maisie had greeted her with joy.

Because Hannah had driven two hours to get to the island she'd been reluctant to leave straight away and said so. 'Can I take Maisie for a walk and check out the island?' she'd asked.

'Do what you like,' Moira had snapped. 'As long as you don't bother me. Stay away from the neighbours, too—I won't have you gossiping to anyone about me. Get her back before dark and then be off.'

So Hannah and Maisie had walked for a couple of hours, checking out the windswept wilderness of the island, with Maisie chasing sticks on the beach, racing like a crazy thing, running circles round and round Hannah, making her laugh. Then sitting beside her on the beach while Hannah felt comfort from her big, solid body. Over the ensuing visits, each one received just as coldly by Moira, Maisie had seemed to listen as Hannah had explained homesickness and Ryan's insistence that they weren't over wandering yet, and her increased doubts about a relationship she seemed to be holding onto by her fingernails...

It had been Maisie she'd spilled her heart to when Ryan had left. It was Maisie who'd listened after that last appalling phone call from her father.

Stupid, stupid, stupid.

And now, as she sat before Josh's fire, rubbing

the dog's damp fur, she found her heart twisting with fear.

She needed this dog to live. Please…

And finally Josh was back, filling the doorway. He was a big guy, weathered, tanned. The scar on his face had been stitched well—maybe if he wasn't so tanned it wouldn't have been obvious. He was wearing faded jeans and an old Guernsey with frayed cuffs, rolled to the elbows to show muscled arms. His dark hair, still damp, seemed to have been cut short and then outgrown its cut. It looked tousled, as if he'd used fingers instead of a comb.

A doctor? He looked for all the world like a fisherman.

He tossed her a bundle of clothes. 'Jogging pants, socks and windcheater,' he told her. 'They'll be huge but they're the best I can do. If you're up to it…you said you're a nurse. I'll need your help.'

'What…'

'I can try for a Caesarean,' he told her. 'I've talked it through with someone who knows.' He knelt by Maisie and met her look head-on. 'Hannah, the vet I talked to… Claire…says after this time, and with the shock, chances are we'll lose her, but I'm willing to give it a try.'

She stared at him, stunned. 'Equipment? Drugs?'

'I told you, I'm a man who likes to be prepared.

About two minutes after I moved onto this island a yacht came in too close and hit the rocks. One of the yachties broke his leg. Compound fracture. It was midnight and the two doctors over the bridge are elderly and don't do callouts. It took an ambulance two hours to get here. Meanwhile I didn't have the right gear to keep him out of pain, and I had to hurt him like hell to get the leg aligned to maintain blood supply to his foot. After that I applied for remote status and put together a kit that'll cope with most emergencies. Caesareans for dogs weren't on my list but Claire's done some fast research and I have gear she thinks I can use.'

'Can we?' It was hardly a whisper.

'Hannah, I don't know,' he said honestly. 'She's in a bad way already. The drugs I have all have the capacity to cross the placenta, which must compromise the pups. As well as that, prolonged labour prior to delivery causes maternal compromise. Claire tells me puppy mortality—even maternal mortality—has to be faced. But the only alternative is to put her down now.'

'No! Please.'

'Then I'll need help. Are you up for it?'

'Yes.'

He nodded, then lifted the big dog and turned toward the kitchen. 'Make-do operating theatre,' he told her briefly, and it was as if they were already a theatre team. 'Scrub at the kitchen sink. Two minutes, Nurse, stat.'

She was left to scramble into his clothes and turn into a professional.

He was a professional. Well, almost.

He'd hauled off his ancient sweater and put an apron over his T-shirt. It was white, with printed flames flickering up the sides. The caption read: *Caution: Extremely Hot.*

She blinked and he grinned.

'My older sister has a warped sense of humour.' The smile died. 'She lives in New York now and doesn't see me…as I am. Unsurprisingly it's never been used. I don't have scrubs so this'll have to do. I don't have another for you but the clothes I gave you are clean. There's antiseptic scrub at the sink, clean towels and disposable gloves.'

He motioned to Maisie, who was now lying limply on a sheet on the kitchen table. 'This is the best I can do as a theatre environment. Luckily the light's decent. I've injected morphine. She's far too passive already, but she's going to need analgesia as she comes out of anaesthesia.'

'Anaesthesia?' she queried. She, too, had moved into professional mode. In normal circumstances, on a guy like this, that apron would have her distracted to say the least, but the sight of Maisie lying helpless turned her from a soaked and a pregnant wuss into the nurse she was trained to be.

'I'm using propofol,' he told her.

'You have propofol?' General anaesthetic? In a doctor's bag?

'I told you, I'm ready for Armageddon here. Fixing my injured sailor wasn't pretty. I hoped that by getting my kit together I'd pretty much guarantee never to need it again, but here we are.'

She was thinking ahead, not liking what she was thinking. 'You'll need intubation.'

'I will, and that's where you come in. I have oxygen. I have intubation equipment. I don't have monitors, of course, so it'll be up to you to watch her like a hawk. Not that there's a lot I can do if her breathing fails but…well, let's just hope.'

He'd started working as he talked, rolling the almost limp dog onto her back, working with soapy water and a razor to shave her abdomen. He used slow, smooth strokes, as if he was trying to calm her rather than prepping for surgery. She wasn't reacting. The morphine must have kicked in fast, Hannah thought—or else Maisie was so far gone she couldn't react.

Either way, Josh was moving on, knowing his course.

'I'll also need help with the pups if there are any alive,' he told her. 'I've put towels in the oven, lowest setting with the door open. Claire says the foetal membrane should be removed and the umbilical cord clamped and severed. In a normal birth, the pup's chest is compressed, expelling

fluid from the respiratory tract and stimulating
the first breath. That doesn't work in a Caesarean so it's over to you. If it's not breathing then
rub hard with clean towels to encourage respira-
tion. Claire says rubbing the hair backwards can
help. I also have a suction bulb to clear mucus if
you need it.'

Then he hesitated and his voice gentled. 'Hannah, you do need to be prepared for dead pups,
though. Claire says after this time there's every
chance we've lost them all. Also, we're looking
at multiple births and there's only the two of us.
I'm sorry, but we need to be harsh and fast in assessment, saving the fittest. You can't spend time
on a pup that doesn't look viable if the next one I
deliver looks like it has a better chance.'

She nodded, feeling ill. 'Got it.'

He'd tugged the table close to the kitchen bench
and had already laid out equipment. She checked
it fast. 'You *are* prepared.' Deep breath. 'If I'd
known you were here and had this… If Moira
had known…'

'Moira had every chance to ask for help,' he
said, and she heard anger behind his words. 'She
made bad decisions and you've been left with the
consequences. That's what happens when people
are—' He stopped, the anger she heard building
cut off short. 'Enough. Are you ready?'

She did another fast visual of the equipment,
then headed for the sink.

'Yes,' she told him, slipped seamlessly into the professional mode he'd assumed. The howling wind outside, the weird feeling of being in a domestic kitchen rather than a hospital theatre, the shock of the last few hours, even Josh's crazy apron...they all slipped away.

There was only a doctor, a nurse, and a patient and pups whose lives were in their hands.

She was good.

Professional assessment. Acceptance of limitations of equipment. Of limitations of themselves. Brief questions and then moving on. She helped him set up the IV for fluids without a question, and she moved fast.

She accepted how compromised he was and acted accordingly. The less time Maisie spent under anaesthetic the better her chances, and as for the puppies...they'd be struggling already. He wasn't going there.

He'd expected to help her with intubation but as he turned to help she motioned him away.

'Got it.'

Her voice was solid, grounded, practical, and he had a sudden sense that this woman would never promise what she couldn't deliver.

It was up to him.

Go.

Josh had performed Caesareans during surgical training—of course he had—but that was years ago, and a Caesar on a dog was a very different thing. He found himself thanking his stars that Maisie wasn't a mini-poodle or a chinchilla. At least a Labrador gave him space.

Claire's instructions were still echoing, listened to and held. 'I can stay on the line and talk you through it,' she'd said. 'But, honestly, Josh, you'll need to work too fast to listen.'

One final glance at Hannah, ready with her intubation gear. One final check of Maisie, lying semi-comatose from the combined effect of prolonged labour, shock and drugs.

'Let's get you safe, girl.'

And then there was no time to think, only time to follow Claire's echoing instructions. She'd sent him pictures and they were now burned into his consciousness, almost into his fast-moving fingers.

He made the incision from the bellybutton to the pubis. So far, so good. Now for the foray into the world of Claire's diagrams and instructions.

A dog's uterus split into two forks—horns, Claire had called them. Canine reproductive anatomy differed dramatically from that of humans and he thanked his stars he'd taken the time to study those pictures. Maisie's need had been urgent but going in blind would have been a disaster. Still, he had to work fast.

Carefully he lifted the uterus and incised, just enough to lift the first pup out. This would have been the pup lodged in the birth canal, taking the pressure of the pups behind. One brief look told him it was dead.

He laid the pup in a bowl beside him, his curt nod without looking up a silent communication to Hannah of the outcome.

Next.

The next pup seemed lifeless but not distended. Was there hope? He had no time to assess—that was Hannah's job. He detached the placenta and handed it over.

The next pup moved in his hand as he lifted it clear and the sensation was like a jolt of adrenaline. He handed it over, but in his peripheral vision he saw the second pup had been laid aside.

Damn.

He wanted more fingers. He wanted more assistants.

He had time for nothing.

When he was sure there were no more pups in the first horn he moved to the next. Another pup. Another movement and he heard the faintest of whimpers. He had no time to react.

Another. Two more.

Done.

Seven.

He had the count solidly in his head, checking and double checking that the placentas were all clear. Leaving one inside could spell disaster.

He had no idea how many pups were alive.

Hannah had kicked a chair to the head of the table and was now sitting down. She was still monitoring Maisie's breathing, but in the sitting position she'd been able to lay the pups on the towel on her lap. She'd lifted a hand and received each pup in turn, but he had no idea what was happening with them.

He still couldn't pause to find out. Claire's instructions were still in his head. He needed to close fast, using subcuticular stitching so as to not interfere with nursing of the pups.

'Josh…' Hannah's voice was urgent. 'She's coming round.'

'Let her wake up,' he said, inserting the last stitch. 'I'll take over. Attend to the pups.'

She scraped back her chair so he could access Maisie's head to supervise the removal of the intubation tube. The big dog gagged. Josh lifted the tubing clear, then watched as Maisie's eyes fluttered momentarily—and breathing resumed.

He almost sagged with relief.

But of course he didn't. When had he ever? He knew this feeling, the sudden drop of adrenaline after lifesaving surgery. He'd learned it was momentary—he needed to brace and then move onto the next thing.

Which was the pups.

'How many viable?' he asked.

Hannah had turned to the oven and was gently placing her armload into its warmed interior. He'd made a nest of towels and she was placing them in, one by one.

'Four,' she said softly. There were two wee bodies laid aside on another towel, another in the bowl. She looked back at them in sadness.

'Let me see.' He had an almost overpowering longing for the city hospital he'd trained in, for skilled paediatricians and neonate nurses, for incubators, for at least one staff member for each baby during a multiple delivery.

He checked the three lifeless forms and knew nothing could be done. Gently he laid the first little body with its siblings and folded the towel around them all.

Four out of seven was a miracle all by itself. Aching for more was stupid.

Hannah stood to take over monitoring Maisie, and he knelt by the oven, checking the clamping of umbilical cords, getting rid of the remains of the birth sacs. Getting his head in order.

Four viable pups. One live bitch. It was far more than he'd hoped for.

Finally he stood and faced Hannah.

She looked totally wiped. Her face was as white as a sheet—or whiter.

She was staring down at the towel covering the dead pups, and her body seemed slumped in grief.

Shock must be taking its toll. What she'd gone through, and eight months pregnant herself...

He lifted Maisie down onto a sheet on the floor.

The dog was dazed, stilled by the combination of shock and morphine.

'Stay with her while I organise a bed for her,' he told Hannah. 'I have two dog beds but they're both deemed to be Dudley's and I don't want property disputes. She needs a nest of her own, where the puppies can be introduced to her as soon as possible. Claire says sooner—her instinct to nurse has to be allowed to kick in fast.

She nodded, mute, and almost unconsciously he put out a hand and cupped her cheek. 'Hey,' he said softly. 'You did great.'

'You did greater.' It was a hiccup of a whisper and he knew she was fighting back tears.

'Yeah, and I didn't find a dead great-aunt and nearly get drowned and I'm not eight months pregnant. I performed a Caesarean. All in a day's work.'

'You know, I'm very sure it's not.' His hand was still on her cheek and she lifted her own hand to cover it. 'Thank you,' she whispered.

And, hell, it was all he could do not to take her into his arms and hug her.

Maybe he should. She was shocked, shaking, distressed. Surely any normal human being would have hugged.

But the feel of her hand over his was creating sensations he'd fought for years to overcome. He didn't need this. Contact? Concern? Closeness?

He lifted her hand away and smiled down

into her eyes. Which might have been a mistake as well.

He'd meant his smile to be one of reassurance, a gesture that she didn't need to touch him, to comfort him.

But she met his gaze and the smile faltered. Her eyes were direct, true.

'Thank you,' she whispered, and shifting his gaze seemed a bigger effort than shifting her hand.

'Moving on,' he said, suddenly harsh because there were things happening that he didn't understand—didn't want. 'I'll fetch that bedding. You're in charge, Nurse.'

She managed a smile back at that, accepting his weird foray into professional titles without a murmur.

'Certainly,' she said meekly, but with a trace of a twinkle that warned that in normal circumstances she was anything but meek. 'Anything you say, Doctor.'

CHAPTER FOUR

IN THE YEARS since the accident, Josh's half-sister had been amazing, supportive, loving, full of advice as he'd built this place, but grief was always between them. Finally Madison had cracked.

'I can't stay here, Josh. I have a job offer in New York. I need a clean break.'

She'd left, but not before leaving most of her gear with him. 'You have a huge garage. Why would I pay rental on a storage facility?' So now one side of his garage was packed with boxes, all labelled by his neat-freak sister.

And if his neat-freak sister could see her boxes now she'd have kittens.

He had puppies. Needs must.

Her boxes labelled linen were now empty. He cut the biggest to form a makeshift crate, put it in front of the living-room fire and filled it with Madison's pink towels.

In the kitchen Hannah was watching over an increasingly wakeful Maisie. He lifted the dog and carried her through to the fire. Hannah followed, and blinked as she saw the pink nest.

'Hey, how do we know the pups are girls? Sexist stereotyping? Surely this is risking all sorts of neuroses in later life.'

He grinned, his first relaxed grin of the night. Hannah was smiling, too, teasing, and he thought, Wow, the courage of this woman...

'People who use my garage for storage do so at their peril,' he told her. 'My sister, Madison, has a twisted taste in aprons and a sexist choice of bath sheets. We're stuck with it. Let's get these babies settled and deal with their psychological trauma later.'

He laid Maisie into the prepared crate, then pushed an armchair up beside it. 'You're in charge of supervising,' he told her. 'Sit.'

'Josh—'

'No argument. Sit.'

She sat.

He returned to the kitchen and double checked the puppies. Four tiny pups, each a miracle in its own right.

The sad little bundle to the side was a tragedy, but compared to what might have been... Don't go there, he told himself. The last three years had been all about shoving unwanted thoughts aside—needs must to survive.

He carried the living pups into the living room and cautiously set them beside their mother.

Maisie stirred and tried to look around at them. She made a huge effort and nosed them with interest, then flopped back down again.

The puppies squirmed against her, nuzzled, instinctively seeking what they needed. And found it.

And as they started to suckle, the tension seemed to ooze from Maisie—and from the two humans watching.

Josh found himself smiling. He glanced down at Hannah and she was smiling too. Mistily.

'Oh, Josh…'

'We did good,' he said, and dropped a hand on her shoulder. It felt okay.

More than okay, he thought suddenly. The feeling of peace… The presence of this woman…

Was suddenly disturbing. This didn't make sense.

Why was he thinking about peace? This was a crazy night. The storm was still building. The wind was howling around the house and the crashing of the sea was truly scary.

He thought suddenly of Skye and Mick and their three kids on the far side of the island. They'd been resolute in refusing help, but they hadn't expected the storm to be this bad. This side of the island was slightly sheltered. Theirs… not so much.

But there was nothing he could do now. His truck had rocked with the wind when he'd driven to the bridge, and the track to Skye and Mick's consisted of little more than sandy ruts. They were on their own.

'What's wrong?' Hannah asked, and he realised she'd been looking up at him in concern. He must have been frowning.

'Just…indeterminate worrying,' he told her. 'Something about a cyclone hovering around my house makes even a grown man uneasy.'

'Even a grown woman,' she agreed. 'Josh, the house on the far side of the island…'

'Moira told you about the Fordes?'

'Mick and Skye? I met them once when I was here, walking Maisie,' she told him. 'When your house was in darkness and I needed help I thought of them, but the track looked too dodgy.'

'I saw them earlier today. I asked them to ride the storm out here, but they said they love a good storm.'

'With kids that age?'

'Their decision.' He couldn't stop his voice sounding harsh. Putting kids' lives at risk…

Like he had?

'Hey, earth to Josh,' Hannah said, and he fought to get his face under control. He'd been too long answering. Too caught up in the past— again.

'I guess there's not a lot we can do about it now,' she said.

'Sadly not. Even if we knew they were in

trouble, the truck will never make it there in this weather. And as for contacting authorities… Chopper? Boat? Not a hope. There's no way anyone can reach them until the weather eases. There's nothing to do but wait.'

'Right.' Then she hesitated and then looked… sort of hopeful? 'Josh, I know this is presumptuous when you've been so good already, but would you have what's needed for… I don't know… cocoa? Toast?'

Cocoa. Toast.

This was what he needed. Practicalities to drive other thoughts out of his head.

'When did you last eat?'

'Breakfast. I thought I'd have something at Moira's but there's something about a dead great-aunt that makes food drop down the list of priorities.'

His smile returned. Black humour was almost universal among medics—used as a release. He knew Hannah would be feeling gutted as well as shocked to the core by what had happened, but humour was a defence. He'd seen it time and time again in emergency departments and operating theatres throughout his career, and he knew how much it helped.

It helped now. It helped him.

'Then cocoa and toast are coming right up,' he told her. 'Maybe even something a bit more substantial.' He hesitated. 'Give me a few moments, though. I need to turn the kitchen back into a kitchen.'

'Let me help.'

But again his hand rested on her shoulder, pressing her down.

'No. Hannah, Maisie's still drug affected. She has her puppies and they need to be with her, but she might roll. Claire was firm on the need for supervision post-op, so you're the Maisie Monitor.'

'But—'

'No buts.'

'But Josh, this is your living room. We've just…taken over. Maybe you could put us all in the laundry.'

'Dudley's in the laundry.'

'Dudley?'

'My dog.'

'Oh, that's right. I saw him. Josh, it's his house.'

'So I should put Dudley here and put you and your dog and her babies in the laundry? I can see Dudley agreeing, but not me. Besides, tonight Maisie and her pups need monitoring, possibly all night, which means shifts, and if you think I'm going to spend the night in the laundry…'

'There's no way you're doing shifts. Josh, she's my responsibility.'

'She may well be,' he agreed. 'But I got very wet on your account. You then allowed yourself to be brought to my house, and you're about to partake of my toast and cocoa. Which means you're accepting that I've accepted responsibility for you. Hannah, you're eight months pregnant and you've had one hell of a day. Back off now and let me take over.'

'I think…' she said unsteadily. 'Maybe I already have.'

'Excellent,' he told her. 'Then keep on with more of the same.'

The kitchen was a mess. There was nothing for it but to go through it like a dose of salts. He missed the 'good ole days', he thought ruefully as he cleaned. As a neurosurgeon working in a major teaching hospital, he'd been able to walk from Theatre leaving a small army of hospital staff to clean up. Now he was it. Neurosurgeon and janitor all in one.

The sad little bundle of dead puppies was his nemesis. He looked down at it for a long moment, feeling strangely gutted. Claire had told him to expect them all to be dead, but still…

Since Alice's death he'd been thrown by all sorts of things, some totally unexpected. Now, looking down at the tiny bundle, he felt the grey void surge back.

Move on, he told himself harshly. He'd spent the last three years working out that the only way to rid himself of this void was to block out the world with activity. He'd dived into his research with a fierceness that left his colleagues stunned.

But research wasn't an option now. He carried the little bundle through to the garage. He'd bury it in the morning—or the morning after. By the sound of the wind he might be stuck inside for quite some time.

With Hannah. Who needed feeding.

Activity, he thought gratefully, and his freezer, his microwave and his frying pan co-operated. Half an hour later he was carrying dinner into the living room. Sausages, bacon, eggs, fried tomatoes and toast.

He gave Hannah a plate and hauled a chair up to the fire to join her. She was staring at her meal with astonishment.

'Wow!'

'Chef extraordinaire,' he told her modestly, then spoiled the effect by grinning. He tackled a sausage but she was still watching him, open-mouthed.

'What?' he said.

'Has anyone told you there's a cyclone outside?'

'Yeah, but not inside.'

'So you have everything you need.'

'I hate shopping,' he said simply. 'A once a month supermarket hit, big freezers and a cold store and I'm done. I have three more weeks before I need to worry about starving.' He paused, reflecting. 'Unless this cyclone hangs around. One stranded midwife, one lactating bitch and four puppies might cut our time frame down a bit. Ten days?'

'I'm not staying,' she said hurriedly. 'Or no longer than I must. As soon as the wind dies I'll take Maisie and the pups back to Moira's.' She hesitated. 'Though Moira's body…'

'That might be complicated,' he told her. 'We'll need to contact the authorities. Do you know if she was seeing a doctor?'

'I have no idea.'

'There's a small clinic at Stingray Bay over the bridge,' he said, thinking it through. 'That's where we all do our shopping, so I imagine it's where she'd go if she did see anyone. We need to see if a local doctor's prepared to sign off on her death on the basis of her medical history, or whether we need to call in the coroner. But, Hannah, it'll have to wait. I've just checked the forecast and it's not pretty. The cyclone's moving slowly. You need to accept that you're stuck here for a day or two.'

She closed her eyes. 'I'm so sorry.'

'I'm sorry too—that your dinner's getting cold. Eat.'

She managed a smile and ate, but in silence. He could see cogs working. He could almost see plan after plan being inspected and rejected.

There was no choice. She was truly stuck.

And so was he.

He didn't enjoy visitors. Since Alice's death he'd withdrawn more and more.

'I hate to see you so isolated,' Madison had said sadly as she'd left for New York.

'It's what I need.'

'Yeah, but I hate that it's what you need. Just remember there's a world out there waiting for when you come out the other side.'

'There isn't another side.'

'There is,' she'd said resolutely, and given him the naff apron. 'For when you're ready,' she'd said, and hugged him and left, and all he'd felt was relief at being alone where he could manage his demons in his own way.

But being alone wasn't in the equation now.

'Is there anyone who'll be worrying about you?' he asked Hannah. He eyed her pregnant abdomen with a certain amount of caution. There must be a dad somewhere, but early in his medical training he'd learned to ask questions with care. 'Do you have friends or family who'll be anxious when you don't get home tonight?' He motioned to his phone. 'My satellite phone can call normal numbers. If communications aren't down on the mainland then you can use it.'

But she shook her head. 'It's not a problem. I share hospital accommodation with other nurses, but they'll assume I've hunkered down to stay with Moira.'

'What about at work? If you don't turn up…'

'I won't be missed. I started leave on Friday.'

'Because of the baby?'

'They wouldn't let me work closer to my due date.' She sighed. 'The downside of working in the same hospital as my obstetrician meant I couldn't lie about my dates.'

'Would you have lied about your dates?'

'Of course,' she said simply. 'I want all the leave I can get after the baby's born.' She grimaced. 'I'm just a wee bit skint.'

'Because you're alone?' he asked gently.

She flushed. 'I'm okay.'

'But you're skint. And you don't have anyone worrying about you. So… You want to tell me why an Irish nurse with a hermit great-aunt is eight months pregnant with no one who'll worry if she doesn't come home at night?'

But she didn't react as he expected. Her green eyes flashed sudden defiance.

'That sounds like a counselling type query,' she said, softening her words with a tight smile. 'I've already copped it from our hospital almoner. "So, Hannah, how are you feeling, facing pregnancy alone?" As if it helps, talking about it. So how about you, Josh O'Connor? You want to tell me why an Australian surgeon is hunkered down on a practically deserted island in a house that resembles nothing as much as Fort Knox?'

'It doesn't,' he said, startled. 'Fort Knox?'

'I haven't seen Fort Knox,' she admitted. 'But

this building… Is this what architects call mini-malist?'

'Simple,' he retorted.

'Or austere, bleak, spartan. Every time I visit, this place seems to be blending with the rocks even more.'

'That's what I intended,' he said, faintly pleased.

'To be invisible?'

'I… No.'

'You're hiding?'

'No!'

'Neither am I, but I'm stuck. I can't go back to Ireland. It's here or nothing. So you…is it here or nothing for you, too?'

'You're channelling your hospital almoner?'

'Maybe I am,' she said, and grinned, then rose to gather the plates. 'Sorry. I know it's none of my business. Can I make you a cup of tea?'

'That's my job.' He rose but he rose too fast. She'd stepped forward to take his plate. They were suddenly too close, standing with only a plate between them.

She was still smiling, looking into his face. He saw freckles and wide green eyes and a tumble of fiery curls. He also saw defiance. And courage?

There was a story here. He knew it. Maybe it *was* because he had ghosts of his own, but he knew them when he saw them.

'Hannah…' Involuntarily he put a hand on her

shoulder but the movement was a mistake. She stepped back fast and his hand fell.

'Sorry.' He frowned, his impression of the ghost deepening. Just shadows, he told himself. Ghosts didn't exist.

Which meant Alice didn't exist.

Her smile had completely disappeared. 'I just thought... I don't need hugging.'

'I wasn't about to hug you.'

'No. You touched my shoulder, that was all, but I'm touchy about touch. It comes from living with a bunch of carey-sharey midwives. *Tell us how you feel, Hannah. No, really, let's have a cup of cocoa and you can tell us all about it.* When what I really want is a glass or two of good Irish whiskey and to be taken out to a pub with a decent band.'

'It's a bit awkward getting to a pub right now,' he said apologetically. And the whiskey...'

I know. This baby means I can't drink alcohol.' She sighed. 'So cocoa it is, but not so much of the touchy-feely as we drink it, if you don't mind. I'm over it.'

'Aren't we both?' he said dryly, and her smile returned.

'Then sit,' she told him. 'You're on Maisie watch while I figure out your kitchen.'

'I can make tea much faster.'

'But I need to feel useful,' she retorted. 'You have no idea how much I want that.'

CHAPTER FIVE

WHEN SHE'D WALKED OUT, the kitchen had felt like an operating theatre but there was no sign of the drama that had played out here now. Josh would have had to clear things to make dinner but he'd gone the extra mile. World's fastest scrub! The room was meticulously clean.

And then she thought, The guy's a neurosurgeon. Neurosurgeons were famous for being meticulous.

A couple of times during basic training Hannah had been a gofer during neurosurgery, and she'd been blown away by the skill and intensity during microscopic surgery. She'd watched Josh deliver the pups and and she'd thought, The guy's good. Now she looked around the gleaming kitchen and she thought, No, the guy's a step above good.

But he was a neurosurgeon with ghosts. There had to be ghosts, she decided. Why else was he hunkered down in Fort Knox?

She'd wondered a couple of times about her great-aunt's neighbour but Moira had put her firmly in her place.

'I wouldn't be impertinent enough to ask. There was a woman here when he first came,' she'd admitted. 'But that didn't last. When did it ever? That scar…maybe she hit him. Good luck to her, I say. Men!'

That had been all Hannah had been able to find out, and in truth she hadn't been much interested. But now, thinking of Josh, she found herself very interested indeed.

But it wasn't about the way she'd felt when he'd put his hand on her shoulder, she told herself. Or the feeling when he'd carried her. Or when he'd checked her baby and reassured her, with all the gentleness in the world. Um…surely it wasn't? It couldn't be.

'It's just because we're stuck here together,' she said out loud. 'We might be here for a couple of days. We need to get to know each other.'

Then she grinned at herself. 'Really? Hannah Byrne, you're a terrible liar. He's fascinating. But after these couple of days you'll never see him again. His story's none of your business.'

But… a little voice said at the back of her mind. He asked about me so he wants to know. Fair's fair. And if you're staying, surely you need to establish he's not someone a woman needs to defend herself from with a kitchen knife.

Ooh, who's being dramatic? she answered herself.

She grinned, admitting ruefully to herself that she could be using thoughts of Josh to drive away thoughts of the terror she'd felt only hours before—of her great-aunt dead in the house a few hundred yards away, of the storm, and of the bleakness that seemed always just around the corner.

Her great-aunt had been cold and uninterested, but she'd been family and in some ways that had seemed important. It had been a tenuous link to home, but a link for all that. Now it, too, was gone.

She needed to focus on something else and Josh O'Connor seemed a good substitute. Even a great substitute.

'Okay,' she said, taking a deep breath. 'Let's make tea and encourage the man to talk. See if you can. Go for it, Hannah Byrne.'

Back in the living room, Josh was sitting on the floor, stroking Maisie's ears. Maisie had pretty much recovered from the anaesthetic but the morphine would still be working. Her pups were nuzzling her teats with greedy contentment, she was settled in a nest of fuzzy towels and her eyes were half-closed as Josh's hand worked its magic. She looked…

Pretty close to orgasm, Hannah thought, and why not with a guy like this stroking her head? She bit back a grin and laid her tray on the coffee table.

'Right,' she said. 'Decision.'

'Decision?'

'Yep.' She tossed cushions on the floor and settled beside him, because with cushions, rug, open fire, a contented dog and pups—and this man—where else would she want to be?

'I've decided,' she said as she settled. 'You've asked about me and I've decided to tell you. On condition.'

'On condition?' He looked startled, and suddenly wary.

'Tit for tat,' she said blithely. 'You want to know why an Irish midwife is stuck on Camel Island with no one to ring to say I won't be home tonight? Then I want to know why a neurosurgeon with the skills you have is hunkered down on Camel Island with—as far as I know—no one even worrying that there's a cyclone bearing down on you. Plus you have a very interesting scar on your face, which my Great-Aunt Moira supposed was put there by one angry wife. Or a lover. Either way, her dislike of men said you deserved it. In order to clear your name, I need your story. So here goes, Dr O'Connor. I'll tell you mine and you tell me yours.'

'For heaven's sake... I have no intention of talking of past history.'

'Fair enough,' she agreed equitably. 'Let's do tea and silence. Or we can talk about the weather. There seems to be quite a lot of weather about lately.'

'Hannah...'

'I really don't mind,' she told him. 'But it seems unfair to ask me if I can't ask you.'

His hand stopped its stroking and he turned to look at her.

She gazed calmly back. He had lovely grey eyes, she decided. Deep and calm, but a bit bemused right now. As if he wasn't used to being challenged.

'I guess as a hermit you don't get to talk about your past very much,' she said kindly. 'Maybe it's horrid. But I'm betting it's not so different from a thousand stories I've heard as a midwife. I imagine as a neurosurgeon you hear hardly any stories. Your patients will be nicely under anaesthetic while you operate. Me? I get to hang around women in extremis, sometimes for a long time, and, wow, the stories I hear would make your eyes pop. Not that I pass any on,' she said hastily. 'Button lips, that's me. I take stories to the grave.'

'I watched you try that tonight,' he said, still wary but his mouth twitching into the beginnings of a smile.

'So I did,' she said cordially. 'But I survived,

and I wouldn't mind adding to my store of gory tales to carry to the next dunking. So what about it, Josh O'Connor? I'll go first if you like.'

He stared at her for a long moment. He really did have amazing eyes, she thought. The way they held… The way they searched hers, as if he was seeing inside…

She wanted to look away, but she didn't. She held his gaze and tilted her chin.

'Both or none,' she said.

'You should give me yours for the free board and lodging I'm providing.'

'That's not playing fair.'

'I can be mean when I want to be.'

'You know, I'm almost sure you can't,' she said thoughtfully. And then she sighed. 'But you have a point. That was a great meal and the bath was something else. If you really want to know…'

'Suit yourself.'

'That *is* mean,' she told him. 'To ask and then act like you don't want to know anyway.'

He shrugged and went back to stroking Maisie.

He really didn't want to know? Well, stuff it, Hannah thought, because suddenly the need to tell him the reason she found herself where she'd never thought to be, why she felt so stupid, so isolated, so helpless… It felt overwhelming.

He might not be the least bit interested, but something deep inside was insisting she needed to explain.

* * *

He *was* interested.

Okay, more than interested. He badly wanted to know.

This interest went against everything he'd tried to instil in himself since Alice's death.

Cut yourself off. Don't care.

But Hannah was right. He'd asked, and his question had backfired.

I'll tell you mine if you tell me yours.

She'd no longer demand but fair was fair. Already he was purging parts of his story in his head. He could give her a brief outline, no emotion, just facts.

And then she started talking and he somehow forgot about focusing on his hang-ups and was caught in hers.

So why was she alone?

'I'm not here through choice,' she told him. 'If I had my druthers I'd be back in Ireland.'

'Right,' he said cautiously. 'So why aren't you?'

'Because my family doesn't want me.' Her voice had turned bleak. 'I'm not welcome.'

'Why ever not?'

'In case you haven't noticed, I'm pregnant.'

'I had actually noticed,' he conceded. She managed a smile, but the bleakness was still in her voice.

'But did you notice there's no ring on my finger?' she asked. 'No? Maybe to you it's not important, but in my father's eyes, having a baby out of wedlock is right up there with giving the finger to the Pope. Worse. You know, if I'd had an abortion and told him, no one else knowing, I'm guessing he'd have been appalled but I'd still be welcome home. A few rounds of the rosary beads and we'd move on. But coming home as a single mother... I can still hear my father. "You've brought shame to the whole family, Hannah. Get rid of it, get it adopted, do what you like, but don't bring it near us. Keep your dirty business out of our sight and let's hear no more about it."'

'Ouch.'

'You said it. Ouch doesn't begin to describe the way that made me feel.'

He thought of it for a while, of the hurt, of the long-held prejudices that still had the power to cause rifts deep enough to drive family apart.

'Your mother?' he ventured.

'Mam thinks what Dad tells her to think and there's an end to it. So does my sister. Bridget and I were close as kids, she'd love to be an aunt but she has the spine of a jellyfish. I have a gran who I love to bits but she's in a nursing home in Dublin, not in a position to give me support.'

'But surely you have friends,' he said, puzzled.

'So few people think like your Dad any more.'

'Of course, but Ryan and I have been travelling for so long we've lost touch. Then there's the fact that I'm an Australian.'

There was a pause at that. He looked at her flaming curls, her freckled nose, her green eyes, her almost translucent, very Irish skin. Plus there was her lilting Irish accent.

'I can see that,' he said dryly, and she managed a smile.

'I'm not indigenous Australian, of course, but there's plenty of folk here with my colouring and accent. There's no want of Irish immigrants in Australia. Thirty years ago my family were immigrants, too. Failed immigrants, though. They came, they saw, and they scuttled back home as fast as money allowed.'

'As bad as that?'

'Dad declared it's a place full of heathens whose only God is the sun. He hates the beach, you see, so why he moved to Queensland... It was ridiculous. But they came at a low time in the Irish economy. Dad's a builder and he was out of work at home. Aunt Moira—Gran's sister—was already over here and she talked of how wonderful it was. But by the time Mam and Dad arrived, Moira's marriage had failed. Moira suffered from the family trait of "what will people think?" so just when Mam needed her most, she retired into her hermit existence and didn't want anything to do with my parents. Which left Mam alone. Mam hated the heat. She was dead lonely and after I arrived she seemed to sink into depression. Dad loathed the climate, loathed not having his local mates, his local pub. The experiment therefore failed. Home we went, with the only remaining legacy my Australian passport.'

'I assume that after all this time, you'd have an Irish one as well.'

'Yes, but it doesn't help the money side of it,' she told him, and sighed. 'Okay, let's get the second part—the Hannah-is-an-idiot story—over. You sure you want to hear?'

He could say it was none of his business. He should.

'From the top,' he said, and she flashed him something that was something akin to a glower.

'Okay, but I'll keep it short,' she told him. 'There once was a girl called Hannah who fell in love with a toe-rag called Ryan.'

'A toe-rag…'

'Gorgeous to look at, charming, carefree, all the things my serious, dour family isn't. Ryan wanted to see the world and so did I. I felt so confined at home. Even after I trained as a nurse, Dad seemed always to be looking over my shoulder. I love our village, our community, but I couldn't stand his control. Even when I moved to Dublin he was always finding an excuse to visit, to judge. Oh, the fights we had… And Mam and Bridge…their passive acceptance of his every decree makes me feel ill.'

'So maybe it was part rebellion, but I fell for Ryan and off we went. Ryan's a trained paramedic, so with my nursing training we could find work wherever we went. We lived pretty much hand to mouth, moving from country to country, working just enough to let us travel to the next spot. But we did have fun.'

'After a couple of years, though, I was getting more and more homesick. To be honest, I was also starting to have doubts about our relationship. Ryan's the eternal Peter Pan. Where there's fun and adventure, Ryan's your man, but responsibility…not so much.'

'There's another ouch.'

'You said it.' She gave a wry smile. 'Anyway, instead of going home, Ryan convinced me to come to Australia. "One last adventure," he said, "before we settle down to boring domesticity." I was in two minds, but I made a quick visit home and nothing had changed. The way Bridget was turning into another version of Mam, I couldn't stand it.'

'So we came. "Let's stay for a while," Ryan said when he saw the beaches, the climate, plus the number of Irish in the pubs. "A year in the one place. Will that do for you, Hannah?" I was unsettled, uneasy, but Moira was here and I knew my gran worried about her. I thought I'll have a touch of family. And, as opposed to my parents, I love the sun and the beach. So we applied for jobs and settled—and then I found I was pregnant.'

He was watching her face. Seeing pain.

'So,' he said, cautiously now. 'I assume not planned?'

'Of course, not planned.' That came with a snap of anger. 'What do you think? That's exactly what Ryan threw at me, too. He said, "You planned this!" like I'd planned a murder.'

'Maybe not the best of reactions.'

'Not when he'd brought home a norovirus from his stupid night at the stupid pub with his stupid mates, which I guess is why the Pill stopped working. And it was Ryan who said I was being paranoid when I said not tonight because we needed extra levels of contraception for the rest of the month…'

She stopped, took a deep breath, moved on.

'Sorry. Too much information. I just can't think of Ryan without knowing what an idiot I was, and for how long. One day I'll remember him for all the fun we've had, but not yet. Things are too raw. Because the moment I told him I was pregnant and I wanted to keep our baby, he said, "It's your baby, sweetheart, not mine." I woke the next morning to a note on the fridge and that was the only trace of him left.'

'Oh, Hannah.'

How to respond? A hug in sympathy? He didn't do hugs and, besides, there was enough defiance in her eyes to tell him a hug would be a bad move. For both of them?

She decided for him.

'So moving on,' she said, doing just that. 'I decided I'd go home but I was dumb enough to tell my family about my pregnancy before I booked the flight. Which was probably just as well. Dad told me exactly the reception I'd receive if I went home pregnant without a ring on my finger. Moralistic? You'd better believe it. It seems tar and feathering's too good for the likes of me. No, don't look like that. I've faced it now and I'm staying put.'

'Alone.'

'You know, I'm probably less alone than I'd be in Ireland,' she admitted. Also less needy. There's sense in my decision to stay. The hospital here's short of midwives and they've liked my work. They'll hold my job and I can stay on in hospital accommodation. There's a creche I can use after my baby's born. Plus, because I'm an Australian citizen, I can access your government's wonderful maternity payments. That's made the decision to stay a no-brainer. If I went back, well, I've been away for three years and I'm out of touch. I have hardly any savings. I'd be trying to find a job when I already look pregnant—how likely is that?—and I'd need to find accommodation. You think that'd be easy in my position? This decision is all about pragmatism.'

'But it still leaves you isolated.'

'I have friends here,' she said defensively.

'Friends who won't worry that you're not home tonight.'

'Will you cut it out?' she said, and huffed. 'I'm doing well, thank you very much. I have my life sorted.'

'Except you're lonely.'

'What's wrong with that? You're the one who thinks being a hermit is a great life choice. So there you are, Dr O'Connor. You have my whole life story, or just about the whole if we're not including the Ferris wheel incident of two thousand and six. So what about you? You want to tell Auntie Hannah or are you still being pig stubborn?'

'Pig stubborn?'

'Pig stubborn. Give.'

'I'd prefer to hear about the Ferris wheel incident.'

'That's not going to happen,' she said darkly. 'It was very undignified, and I didn't even have my best knickers on.' She sat back on her cushions and skewered him with a look that said, *Don't mess with me*. 'So now it's your turn. I know I agreed we could make this one-sided but I've changed my mind. Start with the scar,' she told him. 'Not a Ferris wheel? A lover with a kitchen knife? Something worse?'

'Car accident,' he said, grudgingly.

'When?'

'Three years ago.'

'Bad?' She shook her head. 'No, that's a crazy

thing to ask. I can see by your face that it was bad, and it's not the scar I'm talking about. I'm guessing really bad. Life-changing bad.'

'My sister died.'

'Oh, Josh…'

What followed was silence.

It wasn't a bad silence, though, he conceded, as it stretched. The fire was crackling in the hearth, seeming somehow to mute the noise of the storm. In this room, with Maisie's soft ears still under his hands, with the slight smell of newborn puppies, with the faint mewing sounds of their nuzzling… with this woman sitting waiting with her patient, non-judgmental eyes… It was okay.

She was okay.

Where others would have jumped in with horror, with sympathy, she sat silent and waited for him to tell or not to tell. It was his choice and whatever he decided, he knew it would be fine by her.

'My fiancée killed her,' he said flatly, and waited for a reaction. He didn't get one. The wait stretched on until finally she cracked.

'Well, that sounds dramatic but I'm assuming stupidity or mistake rather than malice. You might as well tell me the whole story.'

Her response almost made him smile. Stupidity or mistake…a combination of the two.

'Aisling's a neurosurgeon as well,' he told her. 'A good one. Her father's a politician with clout, and she's always had family money. She's smart, beautiful, witty, and she has pretty much everything she wants in life. And for a while she wanted me.'

'That was…good for you?' she ventured, and he shrugged.

'Good, like Ryan was for you? Maybe stupid doesn't begin to cut it for both of us.'

'Ryan and I had a very good time,' she said, almost defensively, and he shrugged.

'I guess we did, too. We were surgeons at the top of our game. We had money, skill, respect and egos the size of large houses. Aisling also had the car of her dreams, an Aston Martin, arguably the world's most gorgeous four-seater sports car. Don't think the four-seater was because she was thinking of a family, though. She has two standard poodles, one white, one black, who sit in the back of that car like royalty.'

'Yikes,' she said, bemused. 'That's some picture.'

'Yeah, and I bought right into it,' he said grimly. 'To be honest, her image suited my ego as well. Anyway, the short story is we took my little sister out to dinner one night. I have…had… two sisters. Madison's older than me, actually my half-sister. Alice was an afterthought, conceived in a dumb attempt to save my parents' marriage. She didn't—how could she?—but she was loved, mostly by Madison and me. When she was eighteen she came to stay with me while she was on a break from uni. She thought Aisling was awesome, and Aisling played up to her. We went out to dinner one night and Aisling drove. By then our relationship was showing signs of strain. Aisling had Alice to sit in the front and I copped the poodle seat.'

'Ouch.'

'The back seat in an Aston Martin's hardly suffering,' he said with a smile that contained little humour. 'I was tired and I guess I pretty much zoned out. Then Aisling's phone pinged with an incoming message. I couldn't see what was happening, but it seemed Aisling was reading and texting while talking to Alice—and heading straight into oncoming traffic.'

Hannah's breath hissed in. She'd know, Josh thought. Every medic, every paramedic, every cop, every member of every devastated family knew by now that texting while driving was the new 'drink driving' stupidity. He closed his eyes for a moment as horror flooded back, as it had done over and over, for the last three long years.

He thrust it back with an effort. Who wanted to go there? Not him.

'So that's it,' he said flatly. 'Aisling veered at the last minute and the passenger side copped the brunt of the impact. Aisling escaped almost unscratched. I was left with a compound fracture of my left leg, bruises and the laceration you can still see on my face. And the knowledge that Alice was dead.'

'Oh, Josh…'

'So that was that,' he said, forging on grimly. 'Aisling's family spent a fortune on lawyers. She managed to get off with a suspended sentence, which she can ignore and get with her life. But Alice…' He stopped.

'Hell.'

'It is, isn't it,' he said roughly. For a moment he let the ever-present guilt wash over him, the self-loathing for the man he'd been, for the lifestyle he'd drifted into without thought for the consequences. Aisling had been driving but where had he been? Not looking out for his little sister. Not caring enough.

But then his thoughts were interrupted by a piercing howl, starting low but building to a yowl of despair, echoing ghost-like above the noise of the storm. 'Uh oh,' he said, seizing the distraction with gratitude. 'Dudley.'

'Dudley?' she said, startled out of the horror of the story. 'That sounds like the Hounds of the Baskervilles.'

'I've locked him in the laundry, but he hates this weather. Now he's started he may well howl all night.' He eyed Maisie and her pups and came to a decision. 'I thought it'd be better to keep the dogs separate, but looking at these puppies…'

They both looked. The pups were a squirming

mass of patchwork, brown and black and cream. The littlest one had momentarily lost its teat and was squirming to reattach. They had a glimpse of a tiny face, black with tiny brown eyebrows, a creamy white chest and matching paws.

'You know, I'm guessing these might not be purebred Labrador,' Josh said mildly.

'You mean…?'

'Total number of dogs on this island equals two, and Dudley's brown and black. Do we need to be Einstein to figure the rest?'

CHAPTER SIX

IT WAS GOOD to have a distraction. Or was it?

Their combined stories had hurt, though Josh's was far more gut wrenching than hers. She'd watched his eyes and seen bone-deep pain. The scar was stretched tight over his lean, almost sculpted face, but she knew it wasn't the old injury that was hurting. To lose his sister…

She had a sister back home, still living with her parents, but there'd be no use asking for her support. Once upon a time she and Bridget had been inseparable, falling in and out of scrapes but best of friends all their childhood. As adults, though, Bridget had finally caved in to her father's bullying, while Hannah's rebellious streak had seen her move further and further away.

For the last few years she'd felt like she'd lost her, and she ached for her, but at least her sister, her family, were still intact. To have it any other way seemed unthinkable.

She had an almost irresistible urge to lean forward and take Josh's pain-etched face between her hands, to hold him, to hug him close. As a midwife she knew the power of touch. A woman in labour desperately needed someone to cling to, to grab, to swear at, to know they'd be there whatever. If there was no 'someone' then often a midwife had to step in and be that person.

She wanted to step in now, but Josh was looking intently at the puppies and his body language was telling her to keep her distance. His pain was his business.

Another howl echoed above the noise of the storm. Maybe the rising sound of the storm was sending Dudley to the edge of the dog's tolerance.

The storm should be uppermost in Hannah's mind, too, she thought. However, this situation, this man… Josh himself…was enough to drive the threat of the storm to the background.

Josh was focusing on the puppies because he wanted her to move on. Past the pain of his background. To present practicalities.

Or maybe to present mysteries. A golden Labrador with puppies that were golden—with patches of black and brown.

'I'll get him,' Josh said, and headed into the back of the house.

In two minutes he reappeared, and by his side was the dog she'd seen momentarily as she'd arrived. A skinny, black and brown mutt—almost a kelpie but not quite. Josh had him on a short lead. He was cowering against Josh's leg, as if he needed the comfort of human presence.

He took a couple of steps into the room and then stopped. Stiffened.

And Maisie's head lifted.

Another dog. A threat to her puppies?

Apparently not. Dudley whimpered and pulled forward. Maisie's tail thumped up and down against the rug.

Cautiously Josh let Dudley pull him across to the hearth. Maisie's tail still thumped.

Dudley sniffed, nose to nose. His tail, previously tucked coward-like under his chest, tried a tentative wag of its own.

He sniffed the pups.

Josh was ready to tug him away at the first sign of aggression on either dog's part, but there was none. Sniffing done, Dudley flopped down on the hearth beside Maisie.

Both dogs almost visibly relaxed.

'I guess…' Hannah ventured, awed and a little emotional '…we seem to have settled paternity.'

'Right,' Josh said grimly. 'Like I needed that.'

But Hannah grinned. 'Hey, at last, some good news. That means half the puppies are yours.'

'No!'

'Of course they are,' she said, cheering right up. The responsibility for a dog and four pups was already starting to weigh on her. 'Sharing's awesome. Doesn't the dad have to pay until they finish university, or whatever the doggy equivalent is? Do we need to bring in lawyers, or can we reach an out of court agreement?'

'I don't… They're nothing to do with me.'

'DNA testing it is, then,' she said, her smile widening. 'You stand not a snowball's chance in a wildfire of getting out of this one. Spay your dog, Dr O'Connor.'

'He's not my dog!'

'Really?' She raised her brows.

'And he's neutered!'

'Is that so?' she said, trying for bland, but the corners of her mouth twitched into an irresistible chuckle. 'You know, as a midwife I've learned to accept what people tell me about paternity, but in this case… I'll go bail we're looking at the biological parents.'

'Oh, of course they'll be Dudley's,' he said with a groan. 'But half the fault will be Moira's. Why she didn't tell me she had an unneutered bitch…'

'Did you tell her you had an unneutered dog?'

'She knew. And he's neutered.'

'Really?' Her eyebrows gave a polite, disbelieving quirk and he sighed.

'Okay. Quick background. I bought this land two years ago. It belonged to a guy who was a bigger hermit than Moira, and even older. He had an almost derelict hut over the ridge from this place, and he needed cash to settle debts and reserve a spot in a decent nursing home when he needed it. He didn't want to sell but it seemed he had no choice and he'd reluctantly talked to a realtor. I came and chatted and we agreed I could buy, on the condition he could stay where he was for as long as he wanted.

'I headed overseas. My house was built by contractors, well out of sight of his hut. Then, just before I arrived back, his son contacted me to say the old man had had a stroke and was finally moving. The day I arrived he was gone and Dudley was on my veranda.'

She winced. 'A dumped dog.'

'I hadn't even known he'd had a dog,' Josh told her. 'When I went over to the abandoned hut I saw why. There was a stake in the back yard with a kennel, with a circular rut around the stake, trodden a foot deep. It seems Dudley had been pretty much chained full time. The son had obviously unchained him and left. When I saw Moira she shouted at me to do something. She'd been tossing him food since the old man left but she wasn't taking any more responsibility.' He shrugged. 'So I fed him, dewormed him and tried to settle the worst of his neuroses. A couple of months back I finally decided he'd be mine for life and had him neutered, but it seems...' He looked down at the squirming pile of pups. 'Not soon enough.'

'Well,' Hannah said, watching him, thinking... well, thinking good things. 'Well, well. I'm starting to think you're a very nice man, Dr O'Connor.

You're a man prepared to haul drowning women and dogs out of cars. A man prepared to deliver pups by Caesarean at a moment's notice. A man prepared to put a stray midwife up for the night in the face of a truly appalling storm. And a man prepared to take on the responsibility of a litter of unwanted puppies.'

'Hey, I didn't say…' he started, startled, but her smile widened.

'You didn't have to. I'm starting to figure you out. Squishy in the middle is you, Dr O'Connor.'

But then she winced. She'd been nestled on the floor but her back, never friendly at this stage of pregnancy, reminded her that it didn't like being in this position—or indeed any position for very long. And it had been bumped. She'd been bumped.

She felt safer than she'd felt at any time since her toe-rag of a boyfriend had walked out on her, but right now a wash of weariness hit her like a wall. A twinge of back pain became an unbearable ache, and the need to sleep was almost overwhelming.

And Josh saw.

'You're exhausted,' he said, rising, holding his hands down to hers to help her up. 'I shouldn't have kept you talking. Let's talk about puppy custody tomorrow. Right now, it's bedtime.'

'Do you…? Is there a spare bed?'

'There is,' he said, grasping her hands. 'Madison helped design this house and she supervised its furnishings while I was overseas. Which means there's a Madison bedroom that's furnished with every conceivable luxury—at my expense, of course.'

He tugged her up. She rose and was suddenly close. Very close.

Too close?

And, strangely, all at once the storm seemed louder. Despite its ferocity, it had somehow become an almost unnoticed background to the domesticity of the fire, of the meal, of the dogs and the shared confidences. Now suddenly she was aware of the gusts blasting around the building, and of spatters of whatever was being hurled against the roof, against the shutters.

She felt herself shudder. It must be the after-effects of the day, she thought, of the nightmare she'd been through.

And then she felt her knees sag. For heaven's sake, what was happening?

But Josh's hands were holding hers and his hold tightened. His hands dropped to her waist to stop her falling.

What on earth… He was too close—*she was too close*—but she wasn't pulling away.

This man had saved her and he seemed…her rock.

It was as much as she could do not to cling.

Um…whoops? She *was* clinging. Why didn't her knees want to hold her up?

'Hey,' he said softly, speaking into her hair, still holding her strongly. 'You're knackered. I shouldn't have let you sit up for so long. It's bed for you, sweetheart.'

'I'm not… I'm not your sweetheart.' Memories of that appalling note from Ryan…

And he got it. 'Of course you're not,' he said gently. 'Let's put it another way. You're exhausted, Hannah Byrne. Plus you're battered, bruised and eight months pregnant. So let's delineate our roles in the future. For the duration of the surgical procedure we've just performed I've needed you to be my colleague. We've debriefed afterwards, sharing personal confidences that might or might not assist us to move forward in a professional capacity. We've also decided on the welfare status of four newborns with previously indeterminate parentage. But the professional need for Hannah Byrne has ended. She's off duty. She's now an eight-month pregnant primigravida in my care. So, Ms Byrne, as your consulting physician, it's bedtime. Now.'

And before she knew what he was about he'd lifted her into his arms and was carrying her toward the bedroom.

He'd done it when they'd arrived. It had discombobulated her then when she'd been discombobulated already. Now…discombobulated was too small a word for it.

She felt weak, dumb, out of control…and cherished.

And it wasn't such a bad feeling, she decided as he strode down the passage with her in his arms. She had no intention of staying weak, dumb and out of control, but while she was, while her knees were like jelly and while she had the stupid shakes…why not lie back in this man's arms and savour the strength of him? Savour the feeling that she was safe, cared for, and there was nothing she needed to do but submit?

Oh, right. How politically incorrect was that? Helpless maiden being swept up by knight on white charger…

She couldn't help it. She giggled.

'What?' He kicked the bedroom door open and carried her over to the bed. Somehow, using one hand to hold her, he tugged back the covers and laid her on clean sheets. How did he do that?

'You need a horse and a suit of armour and a lance,' she managed, and he looked puzzled for a moment and then grinned.

'I doubt I'd have been able to pull you out of the water if I was wearing armour. And you… you should have been wearing a flowing gown and…what's that thing all good maidens in distress wear on their heads? A mantilla?'

'I left it at home,' she said mournfully, and then

she took his hand and got serious. 'Josh, thank you so much.'

'Hey, that's fine,' he said gently. 'It's not every day I get to play knight errant.'

'You did it brilliantly,' she told him, and then she couldn't help herself. For some dumb reason her eyes welled with tears and she found herself tugging his hand against her cheek. 'I'd be dead without you.'

'Not you.' He stooped and laid a finger on her cheek. 'You'd have saved yourself and your dog because that's the kind of woman you are, Hannah Byrne. Don't you forget it. Now, is there anything else you need?'

'An alarm clock,' she managed, swiping away a dumb tear. 'Give me four hours' sleep and I'll take over the next Maisie watch.'

'I don't have an alarm but I'll wake you.'

'Promise?'

'Of course.'

She eyed him suspiciously. 'Why don't I believe you? Josh, please…'

'I'll call you when I need you,' he told her, and then, before she realised what he was about, he kissed her gently. On the lips.

It was a fleeting kiss. Maybe meant for forehead rather than mouth? It was the sort of kiss a parent might give a child as they said goodnight.

It burned.

Her hands flew to her lips and she stared up at him in confusion.

She saw matching confusion in his gaze. He backed away from the bed as if…he was afraid?

'Goodnight,' he told her, hurriedly now. 'Madison's set up the en suite with everything a guest could possibly want. Feel free to use anything—I know she won't mind. Call me if you need anything else.'

'There's nothing.' Her voice sounded funny. She felt funny. He was at the door, looking like he needed to bolt but he wasn't sure how to. 'I… Thank you. Goodnight Josh.'

'Goodnight, Hannah,' he said, and left and closed the door behind him.

He returned to the living room and sank into the fireside chair. Outside the wind was screaming, but here seemed a cocoon of warmth and safety. Even Dudley, who'd spent the day cowering and whimpering, seemed to have relaxed. He lay a little back from Maisie, enough to give her and her pups room. His eyes were mostly closed, as if in contentment, but every now and then they'd lazily open and glance across at the little family in their pink nest.

Checking on his woman?

That was sort of like *he* was feeling, Josh conceded, as the idea occurred that he'd kind of like

Hannah to be settled on the settee, here in this room, so he could watch over her, too.

Which was crazy. Hannah wasn't recovering from an anaesthetic. There was no risk to her baby.

Why did he feel so protective?

It was natural, he told himself. He'd hauled her out of danger, she had been in trouble and he was only human.

The storm was doing its best to destroy his house. He was appallingly concerned for Mick and Skye and their children—his helplessness to do anything about their plight was doing his head in. He'd been landed with yet another needy dog, plus four puppies.

His mind stayed stubbornly on Hannah.

He wanted her where he could watch her. The fierceness of the storm made him feel like gathering close everything he cared about…

Cared?

Yeah, okay, he cared, he conceded, raking his fingers through his hair. But only for tonight, no longer. He'd made a vow not to care.

Even Madison… He loved his big sister but Alice's death lay between them like a wall of ice, and there was nothing that could be said or done to break it.

His parents had been disparate, a couple who should never have married. They were currently overseas, his mother climbing an Alp somewhere—he'd need to check Facebook to know where. His father was no doubt doing something important for the government—in Vienna? Or was Vienna last month?

He'd been buying into their life. He'd thought it through over the last pain-filled years, remembering the whole successful surgeon, ego-driven idiot he'd become. He couldn't think of it now without revulsion.

His parents had flown back for Alice's funeral. They'd made a token attempt to be there for him during the worst of his convalescence, but when he'd told them he was managing fine— he wasn't—they'd disappeared again with relief.

His sisters, though, had been his real family. They'd always been a part of him, his core, so of course Madison had stuck around. She'd always be there for him, and he for her, but the pain they saw reflected in each other's eyes was enough for both of them to acknowledge the ice wall.

He only had to glance in the mirror to know how much pain loving another could do. How easily he could get hurt. His wall was his survival mechanism.

Why, tonight, did it seem like he hated it?

It didn't matter. The wall was there.

He rose and poured himself a whisky. Whiskey. Irish. Both Dudley and Maisie watched him cross the room and then come back to them.

'It's okay, guys,' he told them. He stared down into his Irish whiskey and grimaced. 'I know my boundaries. My place is on this side of the wall.'

CHAPTER SEVEN

SHE WOKE TO the sound of crashing. Something was hitting something. Something tinny. Something loud.

It took her moments to struggle out of sleep, to figure where she was, to remember the events of the night before. To remember that this place was built like a fort. That Josh was somewhere in the house, keeping things safe.

Josh. Storm. Banging.

Her room had wide windows but they were strongly shuttered. Chinks of light were making their way through the slats, though. It must be morning.

Josh had been going to wake her.

Had he slept himself? He wouldn't have, she thought. She knew enough of the man to know that he'd have been too aware of the risks of Maisie rolling.

How did she know?

She just did.

But, drat, she'd had enough of his heroism. She

could have taken a dog-watching shift. Did he want to make her totally beholden to him?

That wasn't a kind thing to think, she decided, but as she rose and stomped across to the en suite she was not enjoying the fact that Josh O'Connor was playing the martyr.

The sight of herself in the mirror stopped her short.

She'd taken Josh at his word when he'd said Madison wouldn't mind her using her things. She'd found a nightgown big enough to fit over her bump, and fluffy one-size-fits-all slippers. Josh's bathrobe—she guessed it had to be his because it was brown and anything belonging to Madison seemed to be pink or lavender—made her look almost respectable. She was a bit sore here and there, but mostly she felt fine.

She didn't look even close to fine.

Her car's airbag had gone off as the bridge had tumbled. It had slammed into her face, and she'd had to fight it off as she'd struggled to get out. There'd been timbers at head height.

Her face was a myriad of scratches and bruises.

If she'd been a nurse on duty and someone like her had arrived in Casualty, she'd have been calling for back-up.

It was all superficial, though, she thought, studying bruises and scratches with a professional eye. Bruises always looked worse the day after.

There was nothing there to excuse Josh from his promise to wake her for puppy sentry duty.

Except she was eight months pregnant.

Again her professional self intervened to give her a lecture. If the roles were reversed she'd have broken her promise, too.

It didn't make her feel any less guilty, though. He'd put his life at risk by saving her. Her dog, her problems, had had him sit up all night.

She wouldn't yell at him. She'd just go out and tell him to get some sleep now.

She tucked his bathrobe more securely around her bump. It really was the most gorgeous bathrobe—and did it smell ever so slightly of him? Whatever, for some dumb reason it made her feel…hugged? Maybe that was too big a word but, whatever, she felt not only warmer in it but safer.

Chiding herself for ridiculous thoughts, she headed out to the living room.

The fire was burning low and the dogs were soundly asleep, Maisie in her nest, Dudley just out of it but his nose almost touching Maisie's.

Four tiny, blind worms of puppies were lying peacefully attached to their mother's teats. A family of dogs, seemingly utterly content.

No Josh.

She frowned.

The dogs woke as she opened the door, raised their heads to look a polite enquiry. Nothing to see here, their look said. Maisie knew her well, and Dudley had obviously accepted her as part of the furniture. Two tails gave perfunctory wags and they returned to the important task of sleeping.

Hannah smiled. Maisie's instant alertness, her tail wag and then her contented return to sleep told her the effects of the anaesthetic were well past. They looked like dogs who needed nothing.

So had Josh headed to bed?

She made her way cautiously back down the passage. His bedroom door stood open.

No Josh.

His bedroom was an almost complete opposite to Madison's. The bed was made with military precision. There were no paintings. No photographs. Nothing personal.

She took a fast mental tour back through his house, remembering only tasteful prints. The unknown Madison, she thought, imagining Josh's older sister leafing through online catalogues while Josh let her do as she willed. She could almost hear his brief—'nothing personal, nothing that hurt too much to remember.'

She thought back to her own cramped room, her nursing accommodation. Yes, her family had hurt her, but still every spare inch was covered with memories, of friends as well as family. She hadn't been able to stick things on the walls so she'd bought sheets of plaster board and propped them up so she had almost enough space to fit every face she wanted to remember.

This chopping off of his past…it seemed almost like an amputation. She thought of patients she'd nursed in the past after losing limbs. Of phantom pain that stayed with them for ever.

Oh, Josh…

But where was he?

She walked through to an empty kitchen thinking, had he gone to try and help the artists on the far side of the island? Surely not. She wasn't even game to open a door to see what was happening.

But she did head to the internal door leading to the garage—just to check—and drew in her breath as she saw the space where his truck should be.

Oh, hell. More heroics?

But even as she thought it, the remote-controlled door started swinging upwards and she had to retreat as a blast of wind almost knocked her back into the house.

She waited, knowing he had to have time to drive in and close the door to give him a weather seal so he could get into the house. What she wanted, though, was to rush out and…

And what? Yell, that's what.

He'd put himself in harm's way. Without her. Josh.

She hardly knew the man. What was she about,

leaning against the wall, her body shaking as if she'd been in danger herself, all over again.

The sounds of the wind blasting into the garage ceased. The truck door slammed and seconds later Josh opened the door into the house.

He looked appalling. He was wearing the same pants and sweater he'd been wearing the night before but they were soaked and coated with debris. His deep black hair, wavy when she'd last seen it, was standing almost upright. His scar was almost disguised by grime.

He'd opened the door with his left hand. His right was held tight against his sweater, and she could see bright crimson welling underneath.

'What the hell have you been doing?' Okay, that was not the way she'd been trained to react to injury. She should be calmly neutral, non-judgmental—whatever—but she was still shaking and her professional self had deserted her.

'Being dumb,' he told her, and then he grinned. 'But wow it's wild outside. There's a massage place in town that advertises salt scrubs. They should ship clients over here right now.'

His eyes were smiling, encouraging her to relax. Her voice had been shrill. Verging on hysterics? She took a deep breath and tried again.

'So you thought you'd pop out and see what hundred-mile-an-hour wind feels like? Josh, what have you done to your hand?'

'Cut it on tin,' he said, ruefully, glancing down

at his blood-soaked sweater. 'I did it just then. A sheet of corrugated iron was trying to batter its way against the shutters on the windward side of this place. Left to its own devices, it might have pierced them.' His smile appeared again, reassuring despite the filth of his face. 'Nothing to worry about, Hannah.'

'You went out in the truck—to remove tin?'

'No.' His smile faded. 'I'm worried about Skye and Mick and the kids. The wind's died a little since last night. I thought… I'd check.'

She was watching his hand. The bleeding was sluggish. Instinctively she reached out and caught it.

'Are you sure it's only your hand?

'I'm sure.' He tried to pull back but she was having none of it. A gash was running from wrist down to his thumb. 'It's okay, Hannah,' he said, gently as if she was the one who was hurt. 'It's just blood.'

'Let's get it cleaned up,' she said, a bit unsteadily. 'So, Mick and Skye…did you reach them?'

'No,' he said, gentleness gone. 'The track's washed out and I can't see where to go. The first sandhill saw me bogged. It's taken me half an hour to get back here.'

Anger flooded in, fierce and strong. 'You tried that on your own? You could have been killed.'

'There's a note on the fridge,' he told her. 'I

figured the worst that could happen was that I'd be stuck in the truck until the storm petered out. Which it should do by late this afternoon, by the way. I was safe.'

'Yeah, safe,' she muttered. The cut looked jagged. Dirty. 'This needs stitches.'

'I'll pull it together with Steri-Strips.'

'It needs more than Steri-Strips.' She was trying to lighten her voice, but the shake was still there. 'So isn't it lucky your first rescue was a nurse who has a nice line in needlework?'

'Hannah…' His good hand came up to grip her shoulder. 'It's okay. We're safe.'

'I know I'm safe,' she retorted. 'But for you to do such a stupid thing without me…'

'I'd hardly take an eight-months pregnant—'

'Nurse.' She practically yelled. 'Can you forget the eight-months-pregnant bit? I'm a nurse. Get into the kitchen and let me fix that hand.'

'The dogs—'

'Are fine. Safe, warm, happy. Thanks to you.'

'I wish—'

'Yeah, that Mick and Skye and the kids are the same. I get that. But you've done your best and there's nothing more you can do until the storm eases.' She hesitated. 'You said…this afternoon…'

'I still have satellite connection,' he told her. 'Amazingly the dish on the roof seems to be staying in place so I can see the forecast. The worst of the cyclone went through about three this morning but it's slow in moving away. By this evening, though, it'll still be windy but negotiable.' He hesitated, then added…

'Hannah, I've been onto the authorities. They know of your aunt's death. They also know of my concerns about Skye and Mick. There's nothing they can do, though. No helicopter or boat can get near the island in this weather. And… I checked on your aunt. I've laid her in her bed, covered her, done what I can.'

It took only that. All this and he'd taken the time to give her aunt the decency of dignity in death. Had he known how much the thought of her aunt still slumped in her chair had been doing her head in?

'I… Thank you.' It had almost killed her to leave her aunt. That he'd done this in this storm…

'I figured I had to check on her before I rang the authorities.'

'In case I'd made a mistake?'

'I know you well enough now to accept mistakes aren't your style.'

'Really?' she said, and glanced down at her swollen midriff and winced. 'If you want to believe that…' She took a breath and managed a smile. 'Okay, hold that thought. I don't make mistakes and I'm a very good needlewoman. You have local anaesthetic in that amazing medical kit I saw last night? Everything I need? Then let's get you cleaned up and sutured before I remember just how many mistakes I've made in the past and find myself suturing your hand to your left ear.

He sat at the kitchen table, his hand on a towel. Hannah sat beside him.

She'd brought in a table lamp so she could see better. She had her instruments set out neatly beside her. The local anaesthetic had taken effect, her head was bent over her work and she was concentrating. Fiercely.

It'd be unusual for midwives to suture, Josh knew, but suturing would have been part of her training. Sometimes in the pressure of emergency rooms, with multiple casualties, there was no choice but to hand the job of stitching to a competent nurse.

And she was competent. There'd been no hesitation in the way she'd faced the task, neither had there been hesitation in her use of the anaesthetic. She'd double checked with him, but he had the feeling it was only a formality. Her care with cleaning, debriding and now stitching was as skilful as any surgeon's.

He was no longer watching his hand, though. He was watching her. The copper curls wisping around her face. The smattering of freckles on her nose. The tip of her tongue emerging at the side of her mouth, a sure sign of concentration. Her fierce green eyes…

A woman to be reckoned with.

The unknown Ryan should have had his head read to abandon such a woman, he thought suddenly. What an idiot.

He watched her face, her intentness, her total focus, and he thought…

She was so alone. She needed…

What he needed?

What was he thinking? He dragged his thoughts back into line with a jerk. He was a loner. He'd made that decision and he had every intention of sticking to it. Just because one needy female had crashed into his life in a storm…

Was she needy?

Of course she was. She might come across as fierce and competent, but she could surely use his help.

Maybe he could help her without getting involved himself?

And that was a dumb thought, too. Why was she needy? She'd organised herself a job, accommodation, childcare. She had friends.

Who didn't care for her as they should. She was a woman who deserved to be cared for.

She was tying off the last of the sutures now, and the compulsion to put his hand on those bright curls, to feel them slip through his fingers, was almost overwhelming.

No!

He was tired, he decided. His normal defences

were down and, besides, he didn't even know this woman.

Why did it feel like he did?

Why did it feel like he wanted…?

He couldn't want.

'Right.' She popped a dressing over the stitches and beamed her satisfaction. 'It's a beautiful job if I say so myself. But now, Josh O'Connor, it's time for bed.'

It was so much what he was thinking that he blinked, but her smile wasn't the least bit sexy. It wasn't the least bit…inappropriate. She was smiling kindly, like she'd just patched up a kid with a scraped knee and was telling said kid what to do next. Bed meant just that. Bed.

'Shower first,' she told him. 'But keep that hand dry. Use a surgical glove and hold it out of the water. Then hit your bed and stay there until you've hit the other side of exhaustion.'

'I'm not—'

'Exhausted? Pull the other leg, Josh O'Connor. I'll wake you if I need you. I promise that, and I keep my promises, unlike some martyr doctors I could mention.'

'I didn't promise.'

'I believe you did,' she said serenely, and stood and started clearing the table. 'So what are you waiting for? Go.'

What was he waiting for? He stood, and for

a moment the world rocked a little. He was exhausted, he conceded. But still…

Did he want to go to bed and leave this woman?

'Go,' she said, putting her hands on her hips and fixing him with a glare fierce enough to skewer. 'You're wasting time.'

'Yes, ma'am,' he said weakly.

He looked at those fierce eyes, those dimples, those gorgeous freckles and he didn't want to go at all.

But as the lady said, he was wasting time. It hurt but she was right. He took a deep breath, snagged a surgical glove from the box on the table—and went.

CHAPTER EIGHT

HE WOKE TO the smell of cooking.

Someone…something?…was licking his face. Ugh.

He fought his way to consciousness and shoved. Dudley fell to the floor, rolled, found his feet, put his forefeet back on the bed and started licking again.

'Dudley!' The stern female voice had Dudley glance around briefly, but the dog's tail wagged, with every sign of continuing his display of slavish devotion.

Then Dudley saw the plate on the bedside table and launched himself at that.

But Hannah was fast. She grabbed the dog's collar and was hauling him back before he'd even had time to investigate.

Not that there was anything to investigate. Pre-sleep, when Josh had emerged from the shower, there'd been tea and toast beside his bed. He'd eaten them with gratitude but had slipped into sleep almost before he'd known it. Now all that was left on the plate was crumbs, and Dudley practically drooped with disappointment.

'I'm so sorry,' Hannah said regretfully. 'The catch couldn't have engaged when I—'

'Sneaked in with my tea and toast?' he finished for her. 'You're forgiven. What's the time now?'

'Two p.m.'

He glanced at the bedside table and almost yelped. He'd slept for hours.

'It's lunchtime if you want it,' she told him. 'Cornish pasties. They might not be Irish but I love 'em. That's some food stockpile you have. Every ingredient I needed. Yay.'

'You've been cooking,' he said, fighting the feeling he'd woken in some parallel universe.

'It's what I do when I'm stressed,' she told him. 'And it works for Dudley as well. Maisie's been deserted but I've promised her one—or even two—so that's okay.'

Parallel universe didn't begin to describe the way he was feeling, he decided. He swung back the covers and then thought…hell, he was only wearing boxers. For some stupid reason he was blushing like a girl.

But Hannah wasn't reacting like a blushing girl.

'Hey, nice pecs,' she said, matter-of-factly. 'How's the hand?'

'Fine,' he told her.

'Liar. Use some paracetamol. The pasties will

be done in five minutes.' She hesitated and her smile faded. 'Josh, the wind seems to be dying. I don't know how to work your internet to find out if it'll rise again but I thought—'

'I might be able to get across to Skye and Mick's.'

'I thought *we* might be able to get across to Skye and Mick's,' she said severely. 'There's no I in Rescue.'

'Team talking?' he said, and found himself grinning. She was so sure. So brave. Here she was, eight months pregnant, hauled from a sinking car and yet ready to head out into danger again. 'There's no I in Sense either. The I has to stay home and guard the dogs.'

'The dogs are doing fine without me, and they'll be even better after Cornish pasties. That's a great little courtyard you have, by the way. Though it's a bit small. As the only place they can safely relieve themselves, by the time this wind eases you might find your grass with a hundred burn patches.'

'You're changing the subject,' he growled. 'Hannah, you're not coming with me.'

'It's windy but not dangerously so,' she said serenely. 'The island's not so big that if we get bogged I can't walk home. There's no bridge between here and Mick's. Plus...' Her voice faltered a little. 'Josh, this storm has been terrifying and their side of the island would have borne the brunt of it. If their house didn't hold up I can't think of anywhere safe they could have sheltered. I hope I'm wrong but...well, two medical professionals might be more use than one.'

'Hannah—

'Enough arguing,' she said, as if the argument was indeed concluded. 'Stop distracting me with those pecs, get yourself dressed and into my pasties and then we'll go play Medics to the Rescue.'

The pasties were amazing. He hadn't tasted pasties like this since... When? Since he'd been a kid and his grandma had cooked for him. She'd let him help, he remembered, and weirdly that memory was all wrapped up in the way he was feeling now.

His parents' marriage had been stormy, to say the least. His grandmother's house had been a sanctuary.

This kitchen, with the warmth from the Aga oozing gentle heat, with the dogs nosing around... even Maisie had struggled in to investigate these glorious smells...with this woman wearing his ridiculous apron...

Mostly with this woman, he thought, and had to give himself a fierce mental shake. She's nothing to do with you, he told himself. She's a woman you're helping. Nothing more.

A woman he was helping?

She was giving leftovers to the dogs, washing

oven trays, lifting another batch of pasties from the oven…

He wasn't helping her. *She* was bringing his kitchen to life.

He blinked and tried to focus on his pastie, but the sight of Hannah…

His apron was sitting over her baby bump, its slogan protruding like a neon sign. *Caution: Extremely Hot.*

She was eight months pregnant, battered and bruised. A woman he'd rescued and who needed care. How could she be…hot?

Ridiculous.

'I've made a heap of pasties,' she told him happily. 'Mick and family may well need feeding.'

'If they're okay.' He was struggling to focus on anything other than that crazy apron. And her smile.

'As you say,' she said, her smile slipping. 'Plus they're just as likely to be vegans.'

'Vegans who've been blown to bits by a storm and haven't eaten for a couple of days might well swallow their scruples,' she retorted, but looked doubtfully at her pastie pile. 'I can hardly scrape the meat out now.'

He grinned at her look of dismay. She really was gorgeous.

But she'd moved on. 'Josh, the weather…'

'I checked online while I was dressing,' he told her. Man, these pasties were delicious. 'The wind's easing back a bit. The cyclone's moved out to sea but the edges threaten to blast in again tonight. Not as bad as before, but up to fifty or sixty knots. You're right in thinking we have a window. Maybe three or four hours. The truck's solid. Over and back, collect the Fordes and bring them back again.

'We?' she said, cautiously.

'We,' he agreed. 'As long as you're careful. And follow instructions. And don't do anything that'll put either you or your baby at risk.'

'Yes, Doctor,' she said meekly, but she was smiling and he thought there was nothing meek about this woman.

Nothing meek at all.

The island itself was a mess. Low-growing salt bush had been wrenched and hurled across the island in great tangled heaps. The sand had shifted, so there were vast ridges that hadn't been there before.

He drove cautiously down to the stone wharf and then along the shoreline. The wharf had been used to supply the lighthouse in days when lighthouse keepers had lived here, and it'd been used to land building supplies for his house. It'd be needed again now, he thought—it'd be the only access until the bridge was rebuilt.

Would he need to buy a boat?

But he was getting ahead of himself. Or using the ideas to distract him from what lay ahead.

And from the woman who sat beside him.

Like him, she was concentrating on the track, and he thought she was almost driving for him. He'd seen this look before in fellow medics as they strode toward an emergency room after a call, knowing something grim was waiting, as though concentrating could let them see what lay ahead.

She'd argued with him to let her drive—'Josh, your hand'—but had subsided when he'd told her it didn't make sense, that he knew the island and she didn't. Now, looking at the mess around them, her look was bleak.

'They're sensible,' he told her. 'They'll have found shelter…somewhere. Or maybe the house has held.'

They jolted over the last ridge, and he stopped the truck, staring aghast at the devastation below.

The house hadn't held.

It had been built in a tiny bay, a picturesque piece of magic, with turquoise water and a wide curve of gorgeous sandy beach. When he'd been here in the past he'd been almost blown away by the beauty of the location, and by the simplicity and charm of the wooden cottage Mick and Skye had built themselves.

There was no charm about the cottage now. There was no cottage. The base of the fireplace still stood. A couple of walls did, too, although they leaned drunkenly inwards.

Smashed furniture, clothing, the detritus of living was scattered around the whole bay.

'Oh, no,' Hannah whispered, and he glanced across at her blanched face and wondered if his matched hers.

He could see no one. Where were they?

The wind was still whistling, sand sweeping across the devastation. The sea was a maelstrom of white and grey. Nature reclaiming its own?

No.

Part of him didn't want to go any further. Like that was going to happen. Reluctantly he steered the truck down to the house site, parking in the lee of the tiny amount of protection the chimney gave.

The truck was surrounded by shattered glass, ripped corrugated iron, mess.

'Just lucky Madison left her gum boots,' Hannah managed, striving for a lightness she must be far from feeling. Here was the almost universal black humour medics were famed for, a sole defence when your guts felt like they were being ripped out. She held up a foot to inspect a pink boot with yellow ducklings emblazoned on the side. 'Emergency services, eat your hearts out. Bulletproof vests have nothing on ducklings.'

'My sister got them for rock-pool paddling.

She has a warped sense of style.' Josh's gaze was sweeping the bay, as was Hannah's. Searching. 'Block your ears.'

He put a hand on the horn and blasted, then blasted again. The truck's horn was so loud the sounds of wind and sea faded in comparison.

He stared out again. Nothing.

Where could they have gone?

The Fordes' car, a rickety sedan, was parked away from the house, pointing inland. The windows of the car were smashed and the doors on this side blasted open. Had they tried to leave, then abandoned the car in mid storm? What were their options then?

Had they huddled together to keep safe and then been buried in the mass of shifting sand? He felt sick.

Why hadn't he insisted they stay with him? Why hadn't he picked up the kids and carried them away bodily?

'You can't save people from themselves,' Hannah whispered. 'Josh, you did what you could.' And then she paused. 'Josh, look!'

And at the edge of the curve of the bay, where the sandhills rose steeply, they saw a figure. The blowing sand still formed a gritty fog, but whoever it was was waving.

It was an adult, either Skye or Mick.

'Stay here until I see what's happening,' Josh

said, pushing open the truck door and heading for the sandhill.

'Pigs might fly,' Hannah muttered, and headed after him.

It was Skye on the ridge. Josh reached her first and as Hannah came up behind she saw her fold into Josh's arms. Josh held her tight and hard for a long moment. He'd know, Hannah thought, that the most important thing after terror was contact. Unless someone was bleeding out or not breathing then the reassurance that they weren't alone was crucial.

For long moments he stood and held her. She was dressed in ragged shorts, T-shirt and bare feet. Her long blonde hair was a matted mess, her neck, her legs, her arms a bloody tapestry of scratches.

Finally Josh put her back, holding her tightly by both shoulders, his strength seemingly holding her up.

'You're safe now, Skye. You know I'm a doctor, and Hannah here is a nurse. Where are the others?'

She looked wildly up at him. Her face was as scratched and bloody as the rest of her, but the damage looked superficial, Hannah thought. Her eyes were wild but clear, and her breathing was fast but not shallow.

She saw Josh do a fast visual assessment as well. Moving on…

'Where are they?' Josh asked again, and Skye gave a gulping sob and grabbed his hand and started tugging. Back across the sandhill that'd been hiding her.

He reached back and grabbed Hannah's hand they struggled forward. This storm was no longer dangerous but struggling in soft sand when being sand-blasted was hard. The duck gumboots weren't great footwear. It'd be easier if she took them off but she wasn't stupid—with this amount of debris she'd be another victim in moments.

But she was damned if she was being towed. She gritted her teeth and got her feet moving.

She let her hand stay in Josh's, though. Linking was sensible.

And it made her feel…

Oh, for heaven's sake, she was in emergency mode. Focus on what lies ahead, she told herself, not on the way this man's hand was making her feel.

Then they crossed another sandy ridge and even the feel of Josh's hand faded to nothing.

One man and three kids.

They were crouched in the lee of a rocky crag. It wasn't much of an overhang, though, just enough to deflect the worst of the wind.

The two older kids were holding what looked to be a horse-hair blanket over their heads, forming a canopy to increase the range of the wind-break. A younger child was crouched between them, fists in her eyes, sobbing.

A man lay prone on the ground. A body? Hannah's heart gave a sickening lurch, but then he stirred, groaned and reached out a hand, as if to comfort the littlest child.

'It's okay!' The group hadn't seen them but Skye's faltering cry made them look up. 'Dr O'Connor's here,' she gasped. 'He's even brought a nurse.'

And then she sank to her knees, sagging in a culmination of relief and exhaustion.

The wind was still blasting. The kids looked scratched, battered but mostly uninjured. The littlest one looked a ball of misery but her sobs alone said that there shouldn't be a life-threatening injury.

The man, though... He'd slumped back onto the sand, his face grey. Josh was already slithering down to him.

Triage.

What was Hannah's first priority?

They had one blanket, and for such a group it provided little protection. The kids' faces looked stretched, their eyes too big for their faces, red-rimmed from the sand. Dehydration?

Josh was bent over Mick, focused on his need. Skye and the kids needed her attention, but Josh needed equipment and they all needed water.

She'd seen Josh load a water container into the back of the truck, plus medical equipment. Also, if the truck was here they could use its bulk as a partial wind break. She had no idea what was going on with Mick, but triage said the truck was essential.

'Do you need me now or will I get the truck?' she asked Josh. He didn't look up.

'Truck. We need gear. Drive it around the sand-hill and come at us from behind. Don't try to come straight up and over. Drive slowly, taking the lowest slope rather than the quickest route. If there's any doubt stop and walk back. And, Hannah, treat yourself with care. Take every step with thought.'

He glanced back at her then, as if he was torn about letting her go. It seemed that with all the demands around him, with a myriad of conflicting needs, she and her unborn baby were still in his mix of priorities.

She blinked as their gazes met.

Go with care, his look said, and as she turned and stumbled back to the truck, for some stupid reason she felt her eyes welling with tears.

It was such a small thing, to have someone care as Josh was caring. And it wasn't as if it was personal. It was medical triage.

But it felt personal. For Hannah who'd felt appallingly alone from the moment Ryan had walked out the door, from the time her father had slammed the phone down on her, cutting her off from her entire family—this felt huge.

'So you're overreacting. Go get the truck and stop being ridiculous,' she muttered, but she muttered under her breath because talking to herself with sand blowing into her face was not a good idea. Also thinking of Josh…like she was thinking…was even less of a good idea.

Focus on now. On putting one foot after another into the shifting sand. Her boots were filled. Her feet were ridiculously heavy but it'd be useless to stop and try and empty them. The truck was too far away and Josh needed the truck and its contents quickly.

'So stop thinking and move,' she told herself, but she had a feeling that every part of her, right down to her feet in their ridiculous duckling boots, wanted her thoughts to stay exactly where they kept on drifting.

CHAPTER NINE

MEDICAL PRIORITIES TOOK OVER. Her thoughts
might stray as she struggled back to the truck,
but driving the vehicle across the sandhills took
every ounce of concentration she possessed. They
never had roads like this in Ireland, she thought
grimly. Josh must be really worried to have sent
her to get the truck rather than do it himself.

But she made it. She parked the truck beside
the huddled group, trying to position it to block
the worst of the wind, then hauled open the back
and tugged out the container of water.

She filled a tin mug and handed it to Skye.
'Wash your mouth out and drink,' she told her.
'Lots. Then get the kids to do the same.'

'Mick…' Skye sounded despairing.

'I need to help Dr O'Connor,' she told her.
'We'll take care of Mick. Your job is to get water
into the kids.'

She filled another mug and carried it to Josh.
Whose face was grim.

'I need you to drink a bit of this, mate,' he told Mick, but Mick groaned and turned his head away.

Josh lifted his head, ignoring his clenched lips, the greyness of his face.

'Open your mouth,' he told him. 'I know how much pain you're in but I need to get the sand out of your mouth. Priority, mate. We'll get morphine on board but your airways need to be clear first. Open.'

This was a new Josh. Decisive, authoritative, someone not to be reckoned with. It was no surprise that Mick obeyed.

She headed back to the truck and grabbed the medical bag. By the time she returned, Mick's mouth at least was clear of sand. 'Spit,' Josh was ordering. 'One more mouthful and then we'll let you swallow.'

She set down the bag and then tried herself to assess. The rug was lying over Mick's legs. She lifted it with care and had trouble keeping her face impassive.

Mick had been wearing jeans but they were almost shredded. His legs looked as if something had sliced into him. Both legs looked a bloody mess.

She touched his feet. He was wearing sandals. One foot seemed fine.

The other was distinctly cooler.

She glanced at Josh, his eyes met hers and she knew he was already way ahead of her.

'He and Skye laid over the kids in the worst of the storm,' Josh said curtly, as he held the mug to Mick's mouth again. Mick drank now, but the ashen look on his face didn't change. 'Skye told me. When the house collapsed they headed here and stayed. Mick lay on the windward side all night, bearing the brunt of the wind to protect his family. A sheet of iron slammed into his legs. Deep lacerations and I suspect a compound fracture.'

She nodded, careful to keep her face impassive. Major rule of training—don't scare the punters. She replaced the rug and headed for Josh's bag, using her body to protect its contents from the blowing sand as she searched for what she needed.

'Hey, being eight months pregnant does have its uses,' she quipped to those around her. 'I make a great windbreak.'

There were strained smiles, which was reassuring.

What did Josh need? She forced herself into medical mode, into nurse mode. Swabs. Morphine. Syringe.

The wind was still fierce. The truck wasn't enough to provide protection, and her body wasn't all that great at withstanding its blast either.

Her mind was heading in all directions. Mick's legs had stopped bleeding, but a pool of darkened blood lay in the sand under him. It represented a lot of blood and his colour reflected that. He'd need an IV, plasma, a saline infusion at the very least. And…compound fracture?

She handed over the swabs and syringe and started gathering IV equipment. But Josh stopped her.

'Not here,' he told her. 'There's no way I can get a stable line in with this amount of sand and wind.' He hesitated and she could see his mind working—in a direction he didn't like? But when he spoke his voice was bland. 'Hannah, can you stay with Mick while I take Skye and the kids back to the house?'

'Of course.'

She already knew why. While she'd been battling to get the truck over the sandhill, she'd been thinking transport and she already knew what Josh had obviously figured.

They needed to get these guys to safety—all of them. But the truck was a four-seater for midgets—the back seat was tiny, with a tray at the back. Her first thought had been that Josh should take Mick to safety but then he'd have to return for them, leaving Mick alone. Not safe, not after this amount of blood loss.

Next option. If she took Skye and the kids back to the house first, it'd take her an age to get back, even if she didn't get caught in a sand drift.

Third option. She stayed with Mick and kept him alive while Josh did the first run. It was hardly a safe choice. If Mick was to go into cardiac arrest…

There was no choice.

'There's everything you need in my kit,' he told her, his gaze meeting hers and holding it with a solid message. He meant defibrillator, adrenaline, equipment for resuscitation.

Please, God, don't let me have to use them.

It was a silent prayer but she could see by Josh's face that he knew what she was thinking.

'Just don't go into labour,' he said, smiling with a confidence he must be far from feeling. 'Mick, I'll put a rough splint on your leg to hold it steady, but then I'm taking Skye and the kids back to my house. To safety. We need to make two runs because my truck's too small to fit you all and I want your legs to be stretched out. Hannah's a trained nurse and she'll keep you safe until I get back. My house is solid, warm, with everything we need. You've done a great job, mate. The morphine will kick in any minute. Skye and the kids are already safe. See if you can drink a bit more water, then lie back and let the drugs do their work.'

'Safe…' Mick muttered.

'Yeah, you've done it,' Josh told him. 'Care's now over to me and Hannah.'

'Hannah…'

'She's a nurse in a million,' Josh told him. 'There's no one I'd rather leave you with.'

* * *

The wait for Josh to return seemed to take for ever, but the drugs took hold and Mick seemed to drift in and out of awareness.

He mustn't have slept all night, Hannah thought. He'd been holding his body over his little family, taking the brunt of the storm himself.

'You're a hero,' she told him as she encouraged him to drink more.

'It's Doc O'Connor who's the hero,' he muttered thickly. 'Who'd'a thought a doc would come to this island? Gossip says he's too damaged after that damned accident to work. Doesn't look damaged to me.'

'Nor to me,' Hannah said stoutly, reflecting, not for the first time, how emotional trauma often left a far worse damage than physical. 'We're lucky. He'll stabilise your leg properly and keep you out of pain until we can get you to hospital.'

'You his partner?'

'No.' The idea gave her a sharp jolt. 'I'm Miss Byrne's niece. Josh rescued me as well.'

Luckily Mick was too fuzzy to ask more questions. He lay back and let the morphine send him into a dozy half slumber.

Hannah sat beside him and tried not to feel how uncomfortable she was. Her baby was kicking—hard.

'You don't like being sand blasted either,'

she said under her breath. But then she thought, *Her baby.*

It was an emotional punch. She'd pushed through this pregnancy by putting one foot in front of the other, concentrating on practicalities, but in a few weeks a little person would enter the world. A little person solely dependent on her.

The idea was terrifying.

Would she be able to ring her mother? Her dad would slam the phone down if she tried. Even her sister... She and Bridget had been so close all their lives, but Bridget had caved in, in the face of her father's rage-filled bullying. When Hannah had tried to call, Bridget had whispered his reaction. 'Your sister's shamed us,' he'd told her. 'You'll have nothing to do with her or you'll leave this family as well.' There'd been a few furtive calls but their closeness was gone.

Desolation hit like a wall, but then Mick stirred. She needed to refill his mug—for every mouthful he seemed to spill three—and she went back into putting one foot after another mode.

Finally Josh returned, and with that went any time for reflection. He brought a decent piece of wood, and carefully replaced the rough stick he'd used as a first urgent splint. He administered more pain relief, then they laid the truck's front passenger seat down and manoeuvred Mick aboard.

It sounded simple.

It wasn't.

'Right,' Hannah said at last as she squeezed into what was left of the back seat. 'Home.'

Home.

It was a strange word. A strange concept. Josh was battling to keep the truck on the rutted track. The last thing they needed now was to overturn, but Hannah's hand was holding Mick's wrist and she was watching him, keeping tight obs on his pulse. He could stop being in doctor mode for a moment and let the strangeness of the word drift.

He was going home.

With hangers-on.

When he'd left, Skye had been feeding the kids—there was nothing vegan in the way they reacted to Hannah's pasties. She was staggering a bit, and still dead scared for Mick, but she had her filthy, sand-coated kids around the kitchen table and was doing her best.

'As soon as you've eaten I want you all in the bath or shower,' he'd told them. 'I need to do a full check of all of you but not until the dirt's gone.'

He'd then done a swift dog check. Thankfully his laundry was big. The dogs had been less than impressed when he'd shifted them—Maisie had even given a low growl—but a couple of left-over sausages had done the trick. The last thing he needed was any of the kids venturing into the living room and facing a bitch with pups.

Then he'd headed back to Mick—and Hannah. Now, waiting for him was Skye and three battered children, plus two dogs and four pups.

At home? A sanctuary?

He'd never thought of it as a sanctuary. He'd thought of it only as an escape. Now that escape would be crammed with people he didn't know, kids, dogs, medical needs, dog needs.

And Hannah.

What was there in this woman that made his world seem to settle. That made him feel that, yes, this would be chaos but she'd be there.

He glanced in the rear-view mirror and she saw, she smiled and she gave him a quick thumbs up before turning back to say something to Mick.

She should be frightened herself. Instead she was calm and practical.

When he'd asked her to stay with Mick—at eight months pregnant, the day after she'd almost drowned, after her aunt's death, after terror, while crouching behind a sandhill being blasted by gritty wind, she'd simply said, 'Yes.'

Not even a falter in her calm demeanour.

If he was in the market for a relationship… For a woman…

Which he wasn't, he told himself fiercely, astounded that such a thought could surface at such a time. He put a hand up and traced the scar on his face, as if to remind himself of consequences.

'Are you okay?' Hannah asked from the back

seat. 'Is your hand hurting? Would you like me to drive?'

It took only that. After all this, she was concerned about him.

''We're nearly there,' he said, too curtly, but she smiled.

'That's great, Josh. You hear that, Mick? We're nearly home. Well done, us.'

CHAPTER TEN

THE NEXT COUPLE of hours were focused on medical need and little else.

A clean Skye, draped in Josh's bathrobe, met them as the truck turned into the garage and helped them lift Mick into the kitchen.

'I've put the kids into the big bedroom,' she said, apologetically. 'I hope that's okay. They're asleep already. What can I do to help?'

Her face was bleached white as she looked at her husband. With cause, Hannah thought. With the amount of blood loss he'd suffered, Mick looked dreadful.

'Go to bed with the kids,' Josh said roughly as they got the semi-conscious Mick into the kitchen, onto their rough operating table. 'Skye, you know I'm a doctor and Hannah's a nurse. We have everything we need and there's nothing more you can do. Mick might need you when he wakes up, though, so the best thing you can do now is sleep.'

She left, reluctantly, but she looked almost dead on her feet.

Josh was already inserting a drip. Mick had been drinking but not enough. He needed fluid resuscitation—saline. Josh was swabbing everything three or four times over. The sand was insidious.

The morphine combined with blood loss combined with dehydration was making Mick drift in and out of awareness. As Josh started removing what was left of his pants, though, he groaned and grabbed. Hannah caught his hand.

'You're okay, Mick,' she told him, as she'd told him over and over in the past hour. 'You're safe. Dr O'Connor's good.'

'Mick, we're going to put you to sleep for a wee while,' Josh said. He was inspecting Mick's legs, his face carefully impassive.

Hannah had seen this look any number of times with medical personnel.

Don't scare the patient.

His look scared her.

'Fancy yourself as an anaesthetist?' he asked, and sent her a look she read from years of experience.

'I don't need to fancy myself,' she retorted. 'I'm superb.' She managed a grin and held Mick's hand tighter. 'You have two of the best medical personnel in Australia treating you, Mick. Skilled, professional—'

'And modest,' Josh said, rising to her smile. 'Don't forget modest. Mick, we might have to knock something off your Medicare funding for fixing your leg on the kitchen table instead of in a nice, shiny theatre, but never doubt our ability. Give us a minute to get the worst of the sand off us—we don't want to be shaking sand into our neat handiwork—and we'll have you to sleep and sorted in no time.'

'It still hurts,' Mick faltered. 'And I can't feel the toes on my left foot.'

'That's why we're here, Mick. Leave it to us.

A compound fracture. Multiple lacerations. Compromised blood supply to the foot.

He should be in a major hospital with orthopaedic and vascular surgeons, plus a team of highly skilled nurses, Hannah thought.

There was no such option.

Almost as soon as they had everyone safe in the house the wind started rising again. The forecast was for another few hours' blow. Josh made a fast call, placing them in the queue for evacuation, but there was no chance of that until morning.

Which left Hannah working as anaesthetist while Josh fought to stabilise the fractured leg and, more importantly, to repair the compromised blood supply to the foot.

How he did it with the equipment he had available to him, Hannah had no idea, and she couldn't watch to find out. All her attention was on Mick's breathing, on his thready pulse, on what she had to do to keep both things stable. Anaesthetics were not part of midwifery training. Luckily she'd been in a lot of theatres in her time. She'd paid attention, but still she was well out of her comfort zone. Josh was incorporating her in his scope of responsibility, though, giving curt orders, aware of her tenuous hold on the situation.

Hannah concentrated fiercely on what she had to do—but on the tiny part of her brain that was still capable of other thought, she could only wonder at this man's skill.

He was working fast, obviously acutely aware of the need for minimal anaesthetic when not only was his anaesthetist a midwife, but he lacked any of the superb technology used in modern theatres to monitor the patient's condition. And he was talking to Hannah as he worked, possibly aware that it settled her—at least made her as settled as anyone doing what she was doing could be.

'There are splinters of bone pushing against blood vessels,' he told her. 'The fracture itself seems relatively easy to align but the splinters are doing the damage.' There was a long silence with intense concentration on both their parts, and then a sigh of satisfaction. 'Got it. You b… That one's been kinking the main artery. There's a surge to the foot already.' Another silence and then… 'It's regaining colour. You beauty. I think we're home and hosed, Hannah. Pulse?'

'Still steady,' she told him. Every sense was directed at Mick's pallid face, his breathing, his heart rate.

'Right, let's get the leg splinted before it can shift again. There's more I could do but I don't want to keep him under for a moment longer than I can help. Though I reckon that drip's already doing its job. Amazing what hydration can do.'

That was aimed to make her feel better about the risks. It was true, though. She wasn't imagining it. Mick's colour was already improving.

Josh was splinting, then turning to deal with lacerations. So many…

He swabbed and cleaned and pulled them together with Steri-Strips. 'They'll need decent stitching when he gets out of here, but it's too risky to keep him under for longer.'

His leg was going to look like patchwork for ever.

But there was a for ever, Hannah thought, and she felt almost light-headed. How lucky were they all that Josh had been on the island?

He finished and helped her to reverse the anaesthetic.

'Amazing job, Dr Byrne,' he told her as Mick coughed and choked and then started breathing for himself.

'It's you who's amazing,' she told him. 'To have the forethought to have this equipment here… To have the skills…' She found herself blinking back tears. She thought of this little family and how they'd be if Josh hadn't found them. She thought of where she'd be…

She couldn't help it, she put her arms around Josh and hugged. Hard.

It was the most unprofessional action…

She didn't care. He held himself stiff in her arms but she didn't care about that either. She knew enough of this man to know his ghosts, his pain, his need for isolation wouldn't want her close, but, dammit, she needed to hug him. She buried her face in his chest, she wrapped her arms around as much of him as she could hold—which wasn't as much as she'd have liked because her bump got in the way—and she hugged and she hugged and she hugged.

He hadn't been held since Madison had left, and he hadn't enjoyed being held then. The guilt as his sister had held him had been almost overwhelming.

There was no guilt here. There was only…fear? Fear to hug back? Fear to accept warmth and friendship—for surely that was all it was?

It was also reaction, he told himself. Hannah had had an appalling couple of days. She'd risen to the challenge brilliantly. Her reactions to everything thrown at her had been little less than mind-blowing, and now she was hugging him.

Like Madison, he thought. Madison hugged him to give him comfort and he didn't deserve comfort.

But as Hannah continued to hold he felt more. She was holding and holding, her face was buried in his chest and he realised she was taking comfort, as well as giving it. Almost involuntarily his arms wrapped around her and he found himself hugging back.

He was still watching Mick, but the big man's breathing was settling. His eyes hadn't fluttered open yet but they would.

Mick was safe. They were all safe.

This woman had made it possible.

His head seemed to bend of its own accord, and he found himself letting his chin rest in her hair. He wanted more. He wanted to bury his whole face in her tangle of curls. He wanted to lift her, hold her, protect her...

Claim her.

There was a dumb thought. Primaeval and sexist and wrong on so many levels. Stupid. She was nothing to do with him and she'd be gone tomorrow. He needed to get back to his solitude, to the way of life he needed to keep himself sane.

But for one sweet moment he allowed himself to forget the fears, the promises. He allowed himself to savour the feel of her, the warmth and strength of her hold, the sensation of giving and receiving. Of almost merging.

He could feel her heartbeat. She must be feeling his as well. It felt good. Right. Perfect.

As if it was meant.

But it wasn't meant. It was shock and trauma that had created the moment, and sanity surfaced. He sensed rather than saw Mick open his eyes and he wasn't sure if it was Hannah who tugged away or him, but either way suddenly they were separate beings. Emotion was put away.

They were back to being professionals with a patient emerging from anaesthetic.

'Skye…' Mick croaked. 'The kids…'

And that's what loving's all about, Josh thought as he adjusted the drip and Hannah did the reassuring. It's blind terror, exposure, where someone's death can cut you in two and destroy more than your life.

All he had to do was remind himself of that appalling moment when he'd realised Alice was dead. At the grief etched onto Madison's face.

Solitude.

He needed to get back to it, fast.

He needed to get all these people out of his house. Including Hannah.

Hannah lay in bed and felt guilty. Josh O'Connor was starting to look hunted.

Not only that, his house was filled to bursting. And he must be exhausted.

Skye and the kids were in Josh's big bed. She was in Madison's. Mick was on the settee in the living room. The dogs had the laundry.

Josh was keeping watch over Mick on one of the small fireside chairs. Hardly a base for sleeping. But when she'd demurred, offering to take the first shift, Josh had told where to go. 'Get into bed and sleep,' he'd told her. 'The last thing we need is for exhaustion and stress to bring on early labour.'

He was right, but now… She glanced at the bedside clock. Three a.m. She'd had almost seven hours' sleep. Surely he'd let her now.

But even as she thought it she heard footsteps padding along the corridor. Light footsteps. Skye?

She might be in trouble. Josh had given them all painkillers but they'd be wearing off now.

She could do this for Josh, at least, she thought, and tossed back her covers to intercept her.

She didn't make it. Skye already had the living-room door open and was looking worriedly across to the settee.

The room was lit only by firelight and one small lamp. Hannah could see a shape on the settee—and Josh sitting upright by the fire. He rose as he saw Skye.

'There's nothing to worry about,' he told her

gently. 'I've just put more morphine into his drip but he's sleeping naturally. Everything's okay.'

'I know,' Skye said, faltering. She was wearing one of Josh's T-shirts, Madison's knickers, and nothing else. Her hair was still tangled and wild and she had sticking plaster across one side of her face, but she looked across at her husband and her expression firmed. 'That's why I'm here. I've slept solidly. The kids are okay. They're such a bundle of arms and legs in that bed that they'll comfort each other if they wake. Now I'd like to take a turn watching over Mick.' And then, as Josh hesitated, she held out her hands as if in supplication. 'Josh, I need to.'

And Josh got it. Hannah saw his face soften and she understood. Skye must have thought they could all could die. Mick had covered her and her children with his body. He was her husband and she loved him.

She needed to take a hand in his care.

Josh rose, smiling. 'That's great, Skye. Do you need painkillers yourself? No awards for bravery, now. Yes or no?'

'I could use something,' Skye admitted. 'But nothing that'll make me sleep. I want—'

'To watch over Mick. I understand.' He bent over his truly impressive box of medical supplies and produced a couple of pills. 'take these with water. There's a pitcher here and a glass. If Mick wakes up, see if you can encourage him to drink. The drip will be keeping him hydrated but his mouth was dry so long it'll be like sandpaper. Yours too, I'm guessing. And if there's anything you need, if there's anything worrying you at all, come and fetch me. I'll be in the kitchen.'

'I promise.' She took the pills like an automaton and sank down beside Mick. She took his hand and held it and Hannah and Josh might as well not have been there.

With one last, long look, Josh slipped out of the room. Hannah had backed into the passage.

'In the kitchen, huh?' she said as he closed the door, and she saw him start.

'Hannah…'

'I was coming to offer what Skye's providing,' she told him. 'I've been usurped. But no kitchen for you. You must be dead on your feet.'

'I'm okay.'

'You're not okay. Is your hand hurting?

He'd almost forgotten his hand. 'No.'

'That's great. Bed, then.'

'There's not—'

'A bed? There is. Madison's bed's a double. In you go and sleep. I'll tell Skye where you'll be if she needs you, but she can find me first.'

'Hannah, you need sleep more than me.

'I've had it. I'm fine.'

'You're not fine. Hannah, I will not sleep while you sit up.'

'Ditto for me,' she said serenely. 'Which leaves

one option. We share. I'm going to make myself some tea and toast first, though. Would you like some?'

'I...' He hesitated and then shrugged. 'Yes.'

'Good boy,' she said, and he blinked.

'What, am I a kid?'

'For the purpose of the exercise, yes.'

'Hannah, we can't—'

'Have wild hot sex while sharing a double bed?' She grinned. 'How did I know you were thinking that?'

'I wasn't!'

'What? Not horny as hell over an eight-month-pregnant woman in your sister's stretched-to-bursting too-frilly nightie when you're almost dead on your feet with fatigue? I don't believe it.' Her grin widened. 'But I'll risk it. Go on, get yourself into bed. I'll check the kids and the dogs, make tea and toast, and bring you some. But what's the betting you're asleep before I return?'

She was right. He slept.

She'd taken her time in the kitchen, wanting Josh to settle. Then she'd made him his tea and toast and carried it through to the bedroom.

One look at the unconscious Josh had her returning to the kitchen with the unwanted snack. 'Hey, I'm eating for two,' she told herself with satisfaction, and enjoyed her second snack almost as much as her first.

Finally it was time to return to bed, but a part of her was niggly with unease. Her suggestion to share was surely sensible but there was a little voice saying it was unwise.

'Oh, for heaven's sake, even if we managed to have hot sex there'd hardly be consequences,' she muttered at last, and tiptoed to the bed and slid under the covers.

He had his back to her. Madison's bed was a double but only just.

As she slid in beside him their bodies touched and she felt him shudder.

He was wearing only boxers. His chest, his arms were bare, and she couldn't mistake the tremor.

'Josh?'

No answer. He seemed deeply asleep.

So why the tremor?

She lay in the dark, listening to the storm outside but thinking of this man's history. Of a trauma that had never been forgotten. In the last two days he'd come appallingly close to more tragedy.

There was no weakness in this man. She knew it but she also knew he'd built his armour so his strength could be rebuilt from within.

Not from without. Not by needing people. Not by accepting…care.

She felt the tremor again. There was probably no need for her to intervene, but if this was a nightmare…

Of course it was a nightmare.

She was a nurse. It was her job to care. To stop nightmares.

That was a good, practical way of looking at it, she thought, and before she could think further—because why would she?—she edged closer and wrapped her arms around his broad back. It was a bit tricky with her bump, but it felt okay.

It felt right.

He was still shuddering. She tightened her hold and whispered against his skin, 'Josh, it's okay.' She could feeling her breath waft back at her. 'Everyone's safe. All's well, Josh, love. Sleep, sleep and sleep.'

And for a moment she felt him stiffen. Had she woken him?

'It's only me,' she whispered. 'Your inconvenient friend, Hannah. I'll let you go if you want but, Josh, the kids are safe. Mick and Skye are safe. Even the puppies are safe. You've saved us all. You did good, Josh. Now sleep.'

And blessedly she felt his body relax. His breathing eased, deep and steady.

'Sleep,' she whispered again, and the feel of his back, cocooned against her breast, seemed to have the same soporific effect on her.

She slept.

CHAPTER ELEVEN

JOSH WOKE TO SILENCE. The constant howling of the last two days was gone, and in its place... peace.

And warmth.

He had a woman in his arms.

Hannah.

He had no memory of her coming to bed. Or maybe he did. He recalled a whisper of a sensation, and then her touch, the sound of her soft voice and his dreams abandoning him. Then only sleep.

But somehow in the night he must have stirred, moved, held her in turn.

She was lying facing him, her curls splayed on the pillow, her face lovely in sleep.

Lovely. She truly was.

His arm was lying under the soft swell of her breasts, cradling her. How had that happened?

He was so close he could feel her breathing. He could feel her warmth under her flimsy nightgown.

He felt more at peace than he'd felt for three long years, or maybe even longer. For ever?

Which was crazy. This was the result of exhaustion, he thought, plus the release of the tension and the danger of the past few days.

Sunlight was edging through the chinks in the shutters. Morning. He needed to check Mick.

As if on cue, there was a wail from somewhere in the house, not of distress but of indignation.

'He's finished the Vegemite. I wanted Vegemite on my toast.'

'Uh-oh.' Hannah stirred and woke smiling. Or maybe, like him, she'd been awake and savouring this extraordinary moment. Smiling inwardly even before she opened her eyes. 'Do you not have back-up Vegemite, Dr O'Connor? I call that a major fail. You realise you could well risk a report to the medical board.'

'Not guilty,' he said. He should remove his arm, but it seemed to have no intention of moving. Nothing felt like moving. Here was peace.

Here was…home?

With difficulty he forced his mind back to practical. 'Vegemite's my staple,' he managed. 'There should be two more jars in the storeroom.'

'So who gets up to tell them?'

'Let 'em eat honey,' he murmured, and she chuckled. She had the most glorious chuckle.

But then… 'Mick,' she said, and they both knew the moment had ended. If there'd been any problem, Skye would have come to tell them, but it was over four hours since Mick had had a proper check. And with the wind gone, it was time for the outside world to intrude.

Mick needed medical evacuation—that leg needed to be set by an expert—and they could all leave with him. Skye had told them last night that her mother lived in the city and would welcome them. They could stay with her while Mick recovered and they tried to figure what to do about their ruined home.

Moira's body would be removed by the authorities, to await a coroner's report and burial. With that link to the island gone, Hannah would return to her hospital apartment to await the birth of her baby.

Maisie and the pups were probably officially Hannah's. Could she keep them in her hospital apartment?

Regardless, he'd be left with his solitude. Which was what he wanted.

Wasn't it?

Hannah lifted his arm—with reluctance?—and edged back, rolling to her side so she could read his face.

'Help will come now?'

'We're on a priority list. The sea will still be huge but there'll be choppers. Mick needs skilled orthopaedic surgery to stop permanent damage to that leg. With a death and a serious injury I imagine we'll be top priority. I've said six people need urgent evacuation. Plus there's Moira.'

There was a moment's silence and then…

'Josh, can I stay?'

He stilled. His gut said yes. It was so much what he was thinking.

But then sense took over—of course it did.

'Why would you want to stay?'

She sat up then, tugging the covers up to her breast, as if she was putting distance between them.

'A few reasons,' she said diffidently. 'And before you say no, I'm not asking if I can stay here. Not in your house. But someone has to clear Moira's house and that someone needs to be me. There'll be all sorts of things that need to be organised. And Maisie and her pups… I don't know if I can look after them where I'm living now.'

'It's not safe for you to stay,' he said, automatically in medical mode. 'You're eight months pregnant. There's no bridge.'

'But once the sea settles—and it should settle within the next twenty-four hours—the jetty will be useable. I know there are water taxis at Stingray Bay. I could call one the moment I go into labour. There's a medical clinic at the Bay, so I'd have immediate help, and if a taxi's not fast enough I could get an ambulance to Townsville. And, of course, if the weather even looks like turning again I'd leave immediately.'

'It's a bad idea.'

'It's not ideal but when else am I going to deal with this?' she reasoned. 'After my baby's born? Moira's house will be a mess, and who knows how demanding my baby will be? And there's no one else—Moira cut herself off from everybody. I need to spend a few days here, sorting and cleaning. I'll organise a funeral for Moira over at Stingray Bay, then pack up anything of value, get rid of the perishables, lock it and leave. I've already organised a bigger apartment in Townsville. I just need to get permission to have Maisie there. You know, in the long run Mick and Skye might be interested in Moira's house, but that's for the future. I don't even know what her will says. She might have left the house to a dogs' home for all I know, but for now the responsibility must be mine.'

'You really have been planning.'

'Just a little,' she said, and her face lit with a trace of mischief. 'I wasn't all that tired, and for half an hour or so earlier on you were snoring.'

'Snoring! I couldn't have been.'

'Definitely snoring,' she told him, her smile widening. 'But I wouldn't worry. Extreme exhaustion can make that happen. I hope you're feeling better now. Your hand?'

'It's fine. I'm fine,' he told her, and he had to acknowledge that he was definitely feeling better. Something about the way she was smiling at him…

He had a woman in his bed. In her bed.

Hannah.

Smiling.

For a moment he was totally, absolutely distracted. What he was feeling…

What he was feeling had to be shoved away. He turned away, almost abruptly, and snagged his jeans from the floor, focusing on pulling them on. A man needed to be dressed. A man needed separation.

But her words replayed in his head and he knew separation had to be postponed.

'You can stay here,' he said gruffly, hauling on his T-shirt. 'Here, Hannah, in this house. I have no idea what damage the storm's done to Moira's house…'

'It's a solid house,' she told him. 'Even if there is a bit of damage I can cope, though I might need to borrow some of your supplies. That's why I'm asking your permission.'

'And you might need my help if you go into labour?' He kept his back to her. For some reason it seemed important to keep this impersonal.

'I might,' she admitted. 'I guess…okay, I wouldn't suggest this if I didn't know you'd be here. But I weighed it up and decided that with your support the plan would work. It is asking a bit of you, Josh, so if you say no…'

'I do say no, at least to part of it,' he said heavily, and then he turned back to her. Damn, she was so lovely. Tousled from sleep, in that silly frilly nightgown, her bedclothes pulled up like she still needed defence…

She made his heart twist as it had no right to twist. As he had no intention that it could ever twist.

'If you must stay then you stay here, in this house,' he told her. 'In this stage of pregnancy I'd be needing to traipse across every half-hour to check you haven't collapsed with an antepartum haemorrhage.'

'As if that's likely. You wouldn't have to.'

'I'm responsible, even if you're not,' he snapped, and then regrouped. He was standing now, looking down at her, thinking how young she looked. How vulnerable. How alone.

Do not get sucked in. Do not care.

Too late. He already did.

'You'll stay in this house,' he growled. 'Or you'll leave the island. That's an order.'

'Surgeon ordering nurse.'

'No,' he said, and relented. 'Friend caring for friend. But the choice is still the same. You know I have the room. I can help you with the heavy things, emotional and otherwise. We'll do this together, Hannah, or not at all.'

She gazed up at him and he saw her blink. And then blink again, fast. A single tear trickled down her cheek and she swiped it away with what seemed anger.

'Stupid,' she muttered.

'Me?'

'My emotions. Forget it, I'm over it. Josh, do you mean it?'

'I mean it.'

'Then thank you,' she said gratefully. 'I accept with pleasure.'

After that, events of the day took over. There was little time for introspection, no time to doubt the wisdom of what he'd just promised.

Josh found the Vegemite—seemingly the most urgent of priorities. He checked on Mick, who was still dazed, shocked and hurting.

Skye was in pain, too, with bruising pretty much all over her. She and Mick had protected the kids superbly but at huge cost to their own bodies.

'And I'm about two minutes pregnant,' Skye admitted, and Josh winced. If they'd known that he never would have let her sit up the night before.

'So is everything feeling normal?'

'Actually…cramps…'

'How pregnant are you?'

'I haven't had a check yet, but I think…about eight weeks?'

Damn, why hadn't she said so last night? Josh had checked bruises and lacerations, asked if there was anything else.

Why hadn't he asked about pregnancy?

'Because you're a surgeon?' Hannah said when he told her. 'Don't beat yourself up. I imagine there'll be forms with boxes to tick if any fertile lady comes within your treating orbit. Where are forms when you need them?' She checked and re-assured both Josh and Skye herself. 'There's no sign of an ectopic and you didn't get hit in the stomach. The cramps are easing but we'll take no chances.'

Skye was tucked back in bed, with Hannah reassuring her that with shock and lack of water, tummy cramps would probably have nothing to do with the pregnancy. Regardless, Josh put in a call to increase their need for priority assistance. Without Skye acting as Mum, Hannah and Josh were caught between medical need and the needs of three traumatised kids.

Hannah came into her own here, too. These were good kids, but they were stressed, and Josh watched with admiration as Hannah managed to settle them. She got them baking—'Because I'm Irish and I can't stand toast and Vegemite.'

She made a huge batch of cookie dough, and by the time the medevac chopper landed they were loaded with a tub of Very Weird Cookies.

'For your grandma,' Hannah told them before they trooped across to the chopper. Toby, the eldest at ten, seemed the most traumatised, and with his parents both on stretchers, he gripped Hannah's hand and clung.

'You know your Grandma's going to be at the hospital when the helicopter lands,' Hannah told him, crouching awkwardly to give him a goodbye hug. 'Your mum's on a stretcher because she got more bumps than you, and she's sore. Your dad has a broken leg and a few cuts, but both your mum and dad are going to be fine. The doctors and nurses will look after them, and Grandma will look after you.

'You should come with us,' Toby whispered, unwilling to let go the only security he seemed to have.

One of the medics came across to collect Toby and heard. She smiled down at Hannah, her professional eyes perusing Hannah's obvious baby bump. 'You can come too if you want. You certainly meet our criteria.'

'Thanks, but no,' she told her. 'Josh will look after me, just as Grandma will look after you, Toby, and so will your mum and dad, just as soon as the doctors have patched them up. You've had a huge adventure. When you get to Grandma's, will you draw me a picture of you all at her kitchen table and send it to us? I'll stick it on Dr Josh's fridge. It's a very bare fridge. It needs a picture.'

'Okay,' Toby said, squaring his shoulders a little now he was faced with a task he could handle. 'I'll get the others to draw, too. And maybe Mum when she's better. She paints awesome pictures.' His chin wobbled. 'All her pictures… They'll have blown away.'

'That's one of the reasons Dr Josh and I need to stay,' Hannah told him. 'As soon as you're gone we'll drive over to your house and see how many of Mum's pictures we can collect. There'll be lots of other stuff to find, too.'

'I'd like to help.'

'But your job is to look after your mum and dad and the littlies,' she told him. 'They need you.'

Toby's shoulders squared still more. He sniffed—just once—and then pulled himself together and allowed himself to be lifted up into the chopper.

'Brave kid,' Josh said as they watched it lift in a blast of down-draughted sand. 'And well done, you.' His arm came around her again in an almost unconscious gesture of protection.

She stilled and then consciously removed his arm.

'Well done, us,' she told him. 'Next…'

Next Josh insisted that she rest while he headed back over to the ruined cottage to see what he could salvage. She sort of rested, but not much. Her brain seemed to be wired, as if expecting something else bad to happen.

She wanted to go…home? But where was home?

It felt like nowhere.

The initial chopper was for emergency evacuation but the chopper for Moira's retrieval was different. In the expanse of outback Australia, hearses were useless, and this island was now so remote the same need applied. The unmarked chopper arrived later that afternoon, an official with it.

The official was officious, and apart from a brief question or two to Josh, he wanted to talk to Hannah alone. Josh left them be and returned to desultory clearing up. Sand was everywhere.

When Moira's shrouded body was stretchered to the chopper, he headed back over.

Hannah was standing on the veranda, watching them go.

He did better this time. He didn't put his arm around her. He just stood beside her as the chopper became a speck in the sky and was gone.

'It's all organised,' she told him bleakly. 'Autopsy because she hasn't been to a doctor for years, then, when the death's cleared as being from natural causes, her body will be released to the funeral home in Stingray Bay. He says probably within a few days. I'll let my family know, but they won't come. If it's okay with you, I'll stay on until then and clear Moira's belongings. As long as the sea's settled I can get a water taxi and go back to Townsville from there. It'll hardly be a big funeral. There'll only be me.'

'There'll be us' he told her, and the urge to put his arm around her again was almost overpowering. 'I was her neighbour, and as long as I'm welcome I'll be there.' I'll be with you, he thought but he didn't say it. It wasn't Moira who seemed alone now. It was Hannah.

'It's a shame Maisie'll be too busy to attend,' he told her, seeing her bleakness and aching to drive it away. 'Maisie's the one who loved her, and she loved Maisie. Moira wasn't totally alone. And she knew you cared. Sometimes even a breath of family is enough.'

'Is that what you have now? A breath of family?' She caught herself and dashed her hand across her eyes. 'Sorry. I didn't mean… You don't have to answer.'

He managed a smile. 'It's okay. And my sister Madison is more than a breath. She's a blast.'

'Bossy?'

'You'd better believe it.' But as he said it he thought of Madison's brusqueness and her dictatorial pronouncements and he thought she hadn't been like that before Alice's death. Or not so much.

He hoped she wasn't driving people away with her façade. Had he caused that, too?

'Hey, Josh, don't look like that.' Hannah sounded startled and he realised her bleakness had been replaced by concern. 'You've done good. We've both done good.'

'We have.' But he couldn't get rid of the bleakness fast enough—or maybe he didn't want to, because pain helped him keep the shutters up between him and the outside world. Shutters were important.

And Hannah seemed to sense what he was thinking. That alone was good.

'I might clear up here a bit now,' she said, striving for matter-of-fact. 'I'll start with the light stuff, clearing the fridge and things. I'll come back for dinner. Is that okay?'

'Of course.'

'But something simple. A can of something on toast. Don't you dare go to any bother. Then I'll help with the mess over there.'

'You won't.'

'Then I'll come back here and work until dark.'

'You're eight months pregnant, Hannah. You'll be sensible.'

'Then I'll go to bed,' she said. 'But I won't disturb you any more than I have to.'

'You won't disturb me.' What a lie!

'I already have,' she told him, with a rueful smile. 'I know it and I'm very sorry. It's just a few more days, though, Josh, and you can resume life as you know it. I'm not going to land me or my dog or my pups on you one day longer than I must.'

'Hey, I have responsibility, too,' he said, striving for lightness. 'I concede Dudley's the father.'

'So he is,' she said, suddenly cheerful. 'So we should split the litter down the middle. Dudley gets two, Maisie gets two. As soon as they're weaned I'll bring them back, but I'll do it in the dead of night. I won't disturb you any further. It'll be a true secret baby thing. You'll wake up one morning and there'll be two puppies in a basket at your front door.'

'You'll have your baby by then.'

'So I will,' she said, still cheerful. 'So it might not be me who does the dumping. I hear you can rent a man-with-a-van. Do they deliver puppies? Then there's the issue of no bridge. It'll take some figuring but I'll work it out.

'I'm sure you will,' he said, still in the bleak voice he couldn't seem to get rid of.

'Right,' she said, and visibly braced. 'Next. House cleaning. Off you go and do yours, Josh

O'Connor, and I'll start with mine. See you at dinner.'

And she gave him that same cheerful grin, headed back into Moira's house and closed the door.

She didn't hear him leave. Maybe he was still standing on the veranda.

And she… The smile had slipped from her face the moment she'd closed the door. She leaned against it and it was all she could do not to slump to the floor.

She was shaking all over.

Somehow she managed to get herself into the gloomy living room, sink onto Moira's over-stuffed settee and bury her head in her hands.

It was stupid to shake. There was no reason.

Why did it feel as if she'd just closed the door on her only link to sanity?

'It's reaction,' she told herself. 'It's the storm. Plus half drowning, and rescuing kids and Mick and Skye, and saving the puppies. And Moira's death.'

Moira. She'd been a fiery, hard loner but she hadn't kicked Hannah out when she'd come. Neither had she looked at Hannah's obvious pregnancy with disgust.

Moira had been family. Not much but a little. Now…

Who else did she have?

Almost unconsciously her fingers lifted her phone from her pocket. It had been useless since she'd arrived on the island, it had got wet with the dunking, but suddenly the bars on the front told her connection had been re-established. And she still had charge.

It'd be early morning back in Dublin, she thought. Her family would be awake. Her sister would be about to leave to work.

Dear God, she missed them, and it wasn't just them. It was the village, her town, the whole feeling of belonging. 'I'm too old to miss my mother,' she whispered, but it didn't help.

She phoned.

Her parents still only had a landline. It rang and she waited, imagining her father leaving the breakfast table and heading down the hall. Grumbling. He hated being disturbed before he'd read his paper, but the job of answering the phone was his alone.

'Yes?' When finally he answered the word was a snap.

'Dadda?'

'Is it you?' She heard his breath hiss in. 'Have you got rid of it yet? Your mother wants you home.'

'Could I speak to her?'

'I told you, you're not part of this family until I know it's gone. What do you want?'

'Aunt Moira's died.'

There was a silence on the end of the phone. Then… 'God rest her soul, then, but she's made it clear she's nothing to do with us.'

'Could you tell Gran?'

'We'll not be telling your grandmother. We saw her last weekend and she's slipping.'

Gran. No!

'Da, just how sick is she?'

'Your grandmother's health is nothing to do with you,' he snapped. 'Nothing in this family is until you get rid of whatever shameful thing it is that you're carrying and come home.'

The phone went dead and she was left with bleakness.

During their childhood her father had been a harsh and autocratic parent, a manipulative bully who'd long since turned his wife into a defeated husk. Hannah and Bridget, though, had found ways to have fun despite him. Sometimes it had seemed as if he'd hardly noticed the two little girls who'd learned to be mouse-like in his presence, but as they'd reached adulthood, his need for control had closed like a vice.

Hannah had escaped, to Dublin, to study nursing. Then, as his interference had escalated, she'd left to see the world—with a man she'd fallen for for all the wrong reasons.

Bridget, though, had caved in. 'I'm sorry, Hannah, but I need to stay. I love our village and I love Mam. You're making your own life but I don't have your courage. I couldn't bear the yelling. You and Gran both stand up to him, but I can't. I need my home.'

Home. Where was it for Hannah? Among a pile of cheap furniture in hospital accommodation in Townsville?

What sort of home was that?

She tugged open Moira's curtains and Josh was sweeping sand from his veranda. He must have seen the movement because he raised his hand and waved.

She didn't wave back. The way she was starting to feel about Josh, it was all she could do not to leave this gloomy house and head back over there now. To ask him to hold her. Ask him to give her the comfort she craved.

He'd already saved her life. What else was she asking?

She was asking nothing.

She headed into the kitchen. Josh had already done a cursory clean—when he'd come over the day before to check? There were few signs of the drama that had taken place.

She moved to more practical things. A garbage bag and the fridge. She moved slowly because she ached.

Josh was now shovelling banked-up sand from under the eaves. Surely that wasn't his most urgent task. Was he doing it so he could keep an eye over here? Or to let her know she wasn't alone?

That was fanciful. And she wasn't alone.

Bridget, her sister, would be at work now. She worked for a local solicitor, a friend of their father, and she wasn't supposed to take calls at work. But needs must. She rang and Bridget answered. Cautiously.

'Oh, Hannah, love, are you well?'

'I'm well. Bridget…'

'You haven't had the baby?'

'No.'

'But you'll come home after you've had it? Will you be getting it adopted?'

She sighed. 'No. Bridge, did Dad tell you Aunt Moira's died?'

'Has she?' Bridget sounded distracted.

'He didn't tell you? Bridge, what's wrong with Gran?'

All through their childhood Gran had been their haven, their one true thing. Hannah had been ringing her all through her time away, and she'd been a source of love and comfort through the whole nightmare of her pregnancy.

'She's been losing weight and now they say she has cancer. Terminal. They've just moved her into this hospice place.'

'Oh, Bridge…' She hadn't even known of the weight loss.

'I need to go,' Bridget whispered. 'Love you, Hannah.'

'Bridge…' She cut across her sister's dismissal,

her need urgent. 'Will you send me details of where Gran is and keep me in touch? Please. I need to know these things.'

'Dad says I mustn't.'

'Will you disobey him? For me?'

A deep breath. A sound that could have been a sob but then…

'I will, Hannah. As long as you let me know… when the baby's born.'

'When *my* baby's born.'

'Yes,' Bridget whispered. 'My niece or nephew. Good luck, Hannah. Bye.'

She disconnected.

She could still see Josh on the veranda. Dudley had come out to join him. They were both standing…as if on sentry duty?

It helped.

'I can do this,' she muttered, and rose to fill a bowl to start wiping the shelves. 'I can do this alone.

Especially if Josh was at her back.

'I don't need him,' she muttered, but he was there, and she thought if he wasn't…

He wouldn't be for more than a few days.

'But I'll take what I can get,' she told the empty fridge and started cleaning.

CHAPTER TWELVE

HE TOOK HER back to Townsville. Hannah objected but how could he not? Her wreck of a car was still mixed with the wreckage of the bridge.

Josh's truck was stuck on the island, but he organised a water taxi to collect them on the day of Moira's funeral. All of them. When they reached the mainland he settled bedding in the back, parked it in the shade and left the dogs to sleep while Hannah said goodbye to her aunt.

The service was short to the point of brutal. Hannah and Josh were joined by a director of ceremonies, a couple of funeral parlour employees and an almost empty church.

Hannah clung to Josh's hand during the service—she needed to—but as they left the cemetery she made one last bid for independence. 'Josh, let me take the van. You go back to the island.'

How could he?

'I've hired the van to be returned here,' he

growled. 'How do you think you'll return it if I don't come?'

She bit her lip. 'But I'm so beholden already.'

Which was the last thing he wanted her to feel. This woman had so much on her shoulders.

And when they reached the city he discovered she had more.

Apparently, she'd been sharing an apartment with three other nurses, but she'd made arrangements to move into a bigger apartment, by herself, before the baby arrived. The move was supposed to have happened two days ago and her room in the shared flat was already spoken for.

'We moved your stuff for you. Just collect the key from the janitor,' a bright young nurse told them, eyeing Josh curiously before heading off on her own business. So they found the janitor, collected the key and unlocked the ground floor apartment door.

She was met with her belongings, carried into the living room and no further.

He could tell she was mortified but after one glance she pinned on a bright smile and faced him.

'Josh, thank you. I'll be fine now. If you could… if you could carry Maisie and the pups into the laundry. I think there's a laundry… Regardless, you need to get back. Thank you for everything.'

He looked around the apartment with distaste. They'd walked through a scrappy courtyard to get in so at least Maisie could be let out, but the place itself... Ugh.

It'd be all she could afford, he thought.

Could he offer to help financially? He took one look at her set face and knew how such an offer would be received.

But he could help in other ways.

'I'm staying until you're sorted,' he said, eyeing her pile of 'stuff'. Even her bed was a mess. It had been disassembled for the shift and was now a base, four legs, a plastic bag of bolts and screws that looked ominously small, and a mound of tangled bedding.

'I'll be fine,' she repeated, but she couldn't make herself sound like she meant it.

'Pigs might fly.'

'Josh, no. I can manage.'

'I know you can manage but you don't need to.'

'My friends will help me.'

'I'm thinking your friends are the ones who tossed your belongings in here,' he said grimly, and then he shrugged and smiled. 'Don't make this into a big deal, Hannah. Dudley needs a bit more dad-bonding time anyway. We'll stay overnight, help you get this place in order and then disappear from your life for ever.'

'For ever?' The words came out as an almost instinctive reaction of dismay. He saw the flash of what might have been fear, quickly quashed.

'I'm sorry. Of course for ever. Don't mind me, I'm pregnant.'

'Yeah,' he told her. 'You're pregnant and you need help.' She was three weeks from her due date, he thought, and she was alone.

She was in a hospital apartment. That was reassuring. There'd be midwives and doctors close by, but still…

Apart from a brief stint in basic training he'd had little to do with obstetrics but one thing he did remember was the memory of labouring mothers clinging like a drowning person to their support person.

Who was Hannah's support person? One of the people who'd dumped her stuff in here?

'I'll stay tonight and then leave but it doesn't need to be for ever,' he growled. 'If you need me again…'

'I won't.'

'That's up to you,' he told her. 'You decide.'

It could have been a nightmare. Instead it was almost fun.

She'd been through a nightmare, but Moira's funeral had seemed a marker to end it. She was off the island. Josh had made phone calls to the insurance company and a replacement car was on its way. Maisie was safely delivered. The pups showed every sign of being gorgeous and it should be easy to find them great homes. She had Maisie with her permanently, and she kind of liked having Maisie.

It was almost dark. Josh was staying the night.

Josh was rebuilding her bed.

'Stop it,' she scolded herself, and she darned near said it out loud. This man was a good Samaritan. There was no way that part of her should think… Was thinking…

'No!'

'We have one bolt left over,' he told her and held it up, looking concerned.

'We bought it cheap,' she told him, struggling to haul her disordered thoughts into order. 'Maybe they gave us extra.'

'They're flimsy bolts but they all seem to have a match.' He heaved the mattress onto the base, sat, then cautiously bounced. 'I'm no engineer but it seems sound enough,' he told her. 'I think it should hold.'

'You think?'

'Mattress on the floor, then?'

'No,' she told him. 'Do you know how hard it is for me and my eight-month bump to get up from the floor? What's the worst that can happen? I descend in the night? And, Josh, speaking of nights… We bought our couch second hand and it has springs where there aren't supposed to be springs.'

'Cushions on the floor for me, then,' he said cheerfully. 'Dudley can be my pillow.'

'Josh, you can't.' Oh, her thoughts… Back, girl. 'Maybe you could get a motel?'

'I'm far too clutch fisted.'

'I'll pay.'

'Then you should be more clutch fisted,' he said severely. 'Hannah, I was a Scout. I did camping and everything. I can sleep on two twigs and a reef knot.'

'Really?' She relented and chuckled. 'Okay, cushions on floor, but only if you use some of my pillows. They're my indulgence. I have six.'

'Deal.'

She was still dubious, worrying about it while they made up the bed, unpacked enough boxes to find the kettle and ordered in pizza.'And beer for me because I deserve it', Josh decreed.

Then he decreed that she go to bed. She was, in fact, exhausted.

'I'm heading out to the late-night supermarket to get provisions for breakfast,' he told her.

'I could come.'

'Or you could sleep. What would you rather do, Hannah? Honest?'

She looked into his face and what she saw there demanded honestly. This wasn't a man she could lie to.

'Sleep.'

'Wise,' he told her, grinning. 'Though a bit more risky. If sometime in the night that bed decides it needs its full complement of nuts and bolts…'

'Then I'll descend a whole eighteen inches onto mattress,' she told him. 'Josh, thank you.'

'Think nothing of it,' he told her, and he leaned forward and kissed her on the tip of her nose. 'Sleep. You need it and your baby needs it. Maisie and her babies are already asleep. Dudley and I are in charge of the maternity ward.'

And he chuckled and left her, and she went to bed.

It felt so good, to lie here knowing Josh was coming back, even if it was just to sleep on her living-room floor.

He was leaving tomorrow. For ever?

'Then I'll take tonight,' she told herself, and wished she could take more. Which was an entirely inappropriate thought. She shoved it away with reluctance, and finally she slept.

With her finger just touching her nose.

He came home and the place was in darkness. Dudley watched with interest as he unpacked groceries, but the two mums were asleep.

Dudley got his reward, a bowl of chopped steak. Josh took the same in to Maisie, who woke enough to receive it with canine gratitude. Dudley settled beside her.

Josh came back into the box-filled living room and surveyed the lumpy settee with misgivings.

Cushions on floor, then. He could do this.

Why was he doing this?

Three years ago he'd made a vow not to get entangled with anyone. No one, period. The pain of waking up in a hospital bed to find Alice was dead, seeing the naked grief on Madison's face, being helped into a wheelchair so he could go with her to identify Alice's body in the morgue…

Hearing his big sister's sobs of utter, desolate loss…

Then there were the bleak faces of his parents as they'd flown in for the funeral. The fixed cheerfulness of Madison as she'd determined to get on with her life…

He'd caused it. It wasn't just Josh who was hurting. Pain had washed outward like ripples in a pond. To get involved like that again… To care…

He still cared for Madison—of course he did— but he'd never allow his actions to hurt her again, neither would he enmesh himself in anyone else's life.

The fact that Hannah needed him…

She didn't need *him*. She needed practical help, that was all there was to it. He'd be gone tomorrow, and she could get on with her independent life.

She was like him, he told himself. She'd been hurt and she needed to build her own armour.

In a foreign country, with a newborn baby, with a dog and four puppies…

Only two puppies would be her responsibility, he told himself, and puppies could be rehomed. Hannah could exist with a newborn and a dog. Maternity payments were generous enough for an Australian citizen. She'd get by. She didn't need him.

He rolled over and buried his head into one of her pillows.

Did it smell of her?

He thought it did.

Sleep was nowhere.

She mustn't need him.

He lay in the dark and told himself over and over why what he was thinking was stupid, dangerous, impossible. He knew it was.

And then the bed collapsed.

One minute she was sleeping the sleep of the dead. The next there was a crack of timber and she was unceremoniously tipped sideways. The floor was carpeted. Her fall was little more a slide as the mattress slipped from the collapsing bed. The pillows fell after. Disoriented, she lay where she'd rolled, with a couple of pillows rolling on top of her.

'Hannah!'

Light from the living room flooded in. Her

bedroom light was flicked on and she winced. It wasn't so bad, here on the floor. What she resented more than being tossed unceremoniously out of bed was that light. She wasn't hurt. She had her pillows. Left to her own devices, she'd simply close her eyes again.

'Hannah!'

She heard fear in his voice and it woke her right up. Josh…

'I think I know where that bolt went,' she managed, a trifle woozily. 'You shouldn't have left me in charge of the leg on this side.'

'You're okay?' He was bending over her, his face etched with concern. 'Hell. Hannah…'

'I fell from eighteen inches,' she managed. 'Onto carpet and pillows. Call the fire brigade. Paramedics. Lawyers. I'm sure I can sue someone. This bed's definitely faulty.'

There was a sharp intake of breath and then silence. She heard him audibly regroup.

Her head was still buried in pillows. She should wiggle round and face him but for some reason… well, for some reason she didn't.

'You're sure you're okay?'

'I'm sure.'

'Oh, Hannah…' His voice broke and as it did so a part of her seemed to break as well.

How was it possible that she knew this man

so little and yet so well? She heard his fear. She heard the history of anguish.

'Hey, I really am okay. She turned and smiled up at him. He was bent over her, so near. So near… 'Only I think the rest of the night's going to be mattress on the floor.'

'Right,' he said, and he was suddenly in charge again. Surgeon with a plan. 'Lie still.'

'There's no need.'

'Lie still,' he growled, and she subsided because, to be honest, lying in a tangle of bedclothes and pillows on the carpet didn't seem such a bad fate. Especially when Josh was doing his 'man in charge' thing. She almost smiled.

But he was already busy, hauling the broken bed out from under the mattress and propping the base against the wall, where it stood like a crazy art installation—*Modern Man's Technological Advances in Bed-Making*. Then he stooped and started remaking the 'bed mattress' with her in it.

He tucked in the corners of the bedding. He rearranged the pillows. Finally he tugged the sheet and blanket up to her chin and smiled.

Catastrophe averted,' he told her. 'We'll buy you a new bed tomorrow.' And his smile deepened and he leaned forward and kissed her on the nose.

Again.

On the nose.

And her nose was still tingling from the last time.

His eyes were warm and caring, twinkling with the ridiculousness of the situation but also… well, the caring went deep.

It had no business going deep. She knew he didn't want to care and she didn't want him to care.

Liar.

But the caring wasn't all one way. She looked up into his eyes and she saw concern behind the laughter, and also a trace of fear.

He'd heard the bang as the bed had collapsed and he'd been with her in seconds. This man had seen fear close up and seen the after-effects of it.

Josh…

She was cocooned back in her neatly ordered bedclothes. Josh had ordered her world so she could drift safely back to sleep. While her man watched over her?

Her man.

He was no such thing but, oh, the way he smiled at her…

Enough. A woman had only so much self-control and she'd reached the limit. If it was daylight, if she was properly awake, if this didn't seem like some hazy, amazing dream then maybe she'd have more control, but this was a dream. Josh was so close.

She needed him closer.

Josh.

She put her palms on either side of gorgeous face and drew him down. Was he resisting?

'Josh,' she whispered, and there was no question.

'Hannah,' he whispered back, and then his mouth met hers and there was no space for words.

There was no space for anything but each other.

CHAPTER THIRTEEN

She stirred as the first rays of morning sun-shine glimmered through the sagging venetian blinds. She needed to do something about those, she thought sleepily, but not yet.

Nothing yet.

She was cocooned in the arms of Josh O'Connor and in this space, in this time, who had cares for saggy blinds?

She'd gone to sleep with her arms entwined around his neck—she was sure of it. At least, she thought she was sure. She'd lost herself, totally and surely, the moment his mouth had met hers. Their clothes had somehow disappeared. Skin against skin, they'd seemed to merge, fitting to-gether like two halves torn apart by trauma and now magically come together.

Twin souls.

There was an overstatement, she thought sleep-ily, but she felt her face lift into a smile of warm, sated contentment. Her spine was curved against his chest. At some time during the night she must have turned away from him, which must surely have been sensible as her swollen belly surely couldn't fit breast to chest. But she hadn't been aware of it. She hadn't been aware of anything but her need to be closer and closer and closer…

Sense, though, had prevailed. Sort of. They were both sensible adults—sort of. Their mutual need for warmth, for comfort—for each other?—had only gone so far. Somehow they'd held onto a last vestige of sense.

'I'll not,' Josh had murmured at some time during that sweet night. 'No precautions. Eight months pregnant…'

'You can hardly get me pregnant again.'

He'd chuckled and held her closer, his mouth claiming her, his body doing the same, but the final joining hadn't happened. They were medical professionals. They knew the rules.

Rules, Hannah thought. Where were they now? They had to be reinstated.

She was eight months pregnant with another man's child. Josh had all but told her he wanted no commitment, ever. This was nothing but a night of comfort, a mutual taking and giving before reality inserted its ugly head.

And it was still happening. It was still now. His arms still held her. For a few last glorious moments she could block out the world and let herself imagine this was how life was. For always.

'Awake?' His voice was scarcely more than

a breath and she responded by a tiny stirring against him. Oh, if this was for ever... If this man loved her...

He cared for her. That had to be enough, she told herself. He'd saved her, he'd helped her and this last night he'd held her in what was surely mutual need. He held her still and her body was responding with an almost animal instinct. Here was her place, here was her home.

Here was her man.

He wasn't her man. They were lying on a tumbled mattress on the floor of a sparse hospital apartment. This was *her* home. This was *her* reality. But his hands were holding her spooned to his body, and his mouth was doing something delicious to the nape of her neck.

Oh, the feel of him... The desire to turn and claim what they'd both somehow decided it wouldn't be sensible to claim, to surrender her body totally to his magic...

Except it wasn't her body. It was already claimed, by the child of another man, and they both had the sense to know it. At least she did, but if his mouth kept doing...what it was doing...

'Josh...' she managed, and he released her just enough so she could roll in the cocoon of tumbled bedclothes and look at him.

Mistake. He was so near. He was so... Josh.

'I need to get up.' It was so hard to make herself say the words, but indeed the words were true. She had to somehow tear herself from the fairy story. Someone was kicking her bladder.

'Of course you do,' he said, and smiled, and that smile was almost her undoing. 'Let me help.' He pushed the bedclothes back and rose—and the sight of him…

Dear heaven, the sight of him… What would she give to be taken back in time, to be free, untrammelled, in a position to fight for what she wanted.

She would fight for this man.

Maybe she'd lose—probably she'd lose because he'd made vows for a good reason. Maybe his scars couldn't be mended but, oh, she could try.

But not now. He tugged her up, and as she rose she was achingly aware of the bulk of her body. As he pulled her up, breast to chest, she was still apart from him, pushed away by the bulk of her pregnancy.

History that couldn't be undone.

You need to focus on your baby, she told herself, and as if on cue she felt her belly tighten, and a stab of pain ran across her back.

It'd be a Braxton-Hicks contractions, common in late pregnancy. A reminder that this was no time to add complications to her life.

Complications like Josh?

She snagged the sheet and tugged it around her, then pulled back, aware of an overwhelming desire to weep. She wouldn't. What sort of message would that give him?

'That was some night,' she managed, and somehow she even managed to lean forward and bestow a kiss on his gorgeous mouth. It was a feather touch, no more, a signal to both of them that she understood boundaries and now was the time now to restore them.

'Hannah…'

'Bathroom,' she said, because those stupid tears were welling, like it or not, and she would not cry. 'Then coffee? Have we unpacked coffee yet? There's an imperative. And the dogs… They've been stuck in the laundry all night. Bathroom, coffee, dogs. We need to get this day started, right now.'

And before he could respond she tucked her sheet tighter around her and fled. Into the bathroom where she could close the door, lean heavily against it and figure how to breathe again.

He tugged on jeans and windcheater, wondering how the hell he'd ended up holding a gorgeous, naked Hannah in his arms all night. Wondering how he'd had the strength not to take her as his body had screamed to take her. All the way. Total commitment.

Love?

There was the nightmare. It was both an impossibility and the answer to all his questions.

Quite simply, the way he felt about Hannah was the way he'd vowed he'd feel about no one. That he could love enough to hurt...

He'd seen hurt in Hannah's eyes then. Had she expected to be slapped?

He could never slap her—but hurt her? 'You already have,' he said harshly, out loud. 'You're raising expectations you can't meet.'

So step away now?

He hauled back the memory of opening his eyes after surgery, confused, dazed, seeing Madison's face.

'Alice,' he'd said, and what he'd seen on his sister's face was all the answer he'd ever need.

'And Aisling?' Somehow he'd asked that next.

'She's fine,' Madison had whispered, and the look on her face was a mix he never wanted to see again. Despair. Heartbreak. Blame.

He'd thought he and Aisling were a perfect pair but the risks... What price had his family paid for his stupidity? What price had *he* paid? Pain and pain and pain. Yet here he was, standing in the bedroom of a woman he hardly knew, feeling a tug he'd vowed never to feel.

Be practical! He could help her—of course he could. He could finance a better apartment. He could make her life easier.

She wouldn't let him. It was all or nothing with Hannah—he knew that—and he'd let too much slip for her to forget his backstory. She had her pride. He'd had to work to convince her to take this much.

But he was a friend. Surely she'd let him help.

A friend? The way she'd slipped into his arms last night? The way he'd felt as he'd held her? He could still feel…

No. Memory slammed back, almost like a guillotine. Memory of searing loss. How could he expose himself to that risk again?

A voice in the back of his head whispered, You already have.

'Then back away.' He said it out loud and the sound of his voice jarred him into the present, into practicalities. 'Move on. Get this place organised and then get back to your island. You've played the good Samaritan and nothing else is needed. You can see by her face that she gets the boundaries. Tell her. Talk to her. But whatever you do, get out of here, Josh O'Connor, before every one of your resolutions turns to dust.'

Hannah was still in the bathroom. He could hear the sound of running water.

Hannah in the shower. Her naked body…

'Cut it out!' He said that out loud as well and headed for the laundry to let the dogs out. Hannah's courtyard was minuscule. How could a bitch and four puppies use only this as their outside space? There'd be no lawn left for Hannah to sit in the sun and play with her baby.

That was Hannah's business, not his.

He headed back to the kitchen and rooted through boxes until he found kettle and mugs and coffee. Muesli? Ugh. What he'd really like was a decent fry-up. He'd seen a convenience store last night, only a block from here.

He headed to the bathroom door. The shower had stopped.

'You feel like eggs and bacon?' he called through the door. 'Or would you like to go out for breakfast?'

No answer.

'Hannah?'

'Josh…' And the way she said the word had him pushing the door wide, regardless.

She was bent over the hand basin, gripping it fiercely with both hands. Her sheet had fallen to the floor but she was in no mind to care. Her entire body was rigid.

'Hannah…'

'It's coming,' she managed. 'Josh, my baby's coming. So hard… So fast… Josh, please… Help me, Josh. Help…'

And everything else was nothing.

The contractions were deep and strong right from the start. This was to be no labour where Mum could stay home, rest between contractions, wait until they were five minutes apart and then think it was time they made for the labour ward. Hannah's next contraction came three minutes later, the next two. And in between her body was rigid, fierce with expectation of pain.

And fear. He could see it and he could feel it as he carried her back to the bedroom.

This woman was a midwife. She knew birth almost better than anyone, but right now she wasn't a midwife. She was a first-time mum and she was terrified. Professionalism had gone out of the window.

And Josh?

He didn't feel like a doctor either.

In the time after the accident, when his role had been patient rather than doctor, his fears had been those of anyone facing the unknown. Being on the outside, looking in, was a very different experience from the opposite—surrendering control.

He felt way out of control now. The sight of Hannah in pain was doing his head in. He set her back on their collapsed bed and she grabbed his hands like she was drowning.

'Stay with me,' she managed. It was a fierce order, but it was a helpless plea.

'Try and get rid of me,' he told her. 'I hauled you and your baby out of that car and I'm all for happy endings. You can't throw me out of this movie at three quarter time.'

She managed to chuckle but it was a wavery laugh, turning into a pain-filled gasp. 'Josh…'

'Yeah, whatever's happening's happening fast.' Stupidly he was having trouble keeping his voice steady. He placed a palm on her rock-hard belly as the next contraction started to roll through. 'Hannah, let's get you across to the hospital. By the feel of these contractions, he or she isn't mucking around.'

'I… Yes… I'm booked in…' And then the full force of the contraction hit and his hands were caught again.

Afterwards he'd find scratches where her fingernails had dug into his palms, but he didn't feel pain. He held her, willing strength, willing confidence, willing courage, and she closed her eyes and moaned, and he felt that he'd never been in such a position of trust…

He'd seen births before—of course he had, throughout his training. He'd seen birth partners gripped like this, held, sworn at, shoved away and then grabbed again…

He'd never understood until now that being in this position was an honour above all others.

'You need to let me go, Hannah, love,' he said, gently now as the contraction eased. 'A mattress on the floor with no equipment is scarcely the optimal place to give birth. I need to find you a bathrobe and get you to where you need to be.'

'Us,' Hannah gasped. 'Oh, Josh, please… Get us.'

'Of course us,' he said, and he heard the break in his voice as he said it. 'Hannah, we're in this together. It's you who has to do the work but I promise you, I won't leave you.'

He was there. Somehow he got her across to the hospital but he was still there.

As educated, as prepared as any woman giving birth for the first time could be, nothing had prepared her for this. Her body had been taken over by a force she had no control over. Her contractions had started strong and kept right on, wave after wave of power and pain.

In the birth room with her were two of the hospital midwives, women she'd worked with, women she counted as her friends. She could feel their empathy, their support, their skill.

A doctor flitted in from time to time, muttering things like 'Progressing nicely, keep it up…' The white coat at the end of the bed barely made an impression. It was just the midwives and Josh.

Josh.

She had no right to ask him to stay, but she had no intention of letting him go. *Now* was entirely selfish. She'd take what she needed to birth this baby, to have this little one safe in her arms, and what she needed was strength.

And Josh gave it to her. He sat beside her for what seemed hour after interminable hour. He let her grip his hands in a death grip during contractions. How did that help? She only knew that it did.

He murmured to her. He held her when she needed to be held. He listened to her swear—she didn't even know she knew these words. He was just there.

Josh. Her hold on sanity. Her hold on life.

He was no such thing but that's what he felt like and she wasn't letting go for a moment. And when finally, finally that last moment came...

'One more push.' Josh was right there, firm, sure, her rock in a sea of pain. 'You can do this, Hannah. We can see your baby. Just one more push and you'll have him safe in your arms.'

And she looked up into his face, stern and sure, compassionate, caring, but ruthless in his certainty for what she had to do—and she pushed.

And one appalling minute later she heard a yowl of indignant protest and a tiny, slippery miracle of a baby was lying on her breast. Warm and wanting, mewing a tiny baby sound, already nudging towards her nipple.

'You have a daughter...' Josh's voice was faint, seemingly far away.

'A daughter.' Her focus should be all on this tiny slip of a brand-new person, but it seemed there was room still for that ever-present awareness of Josh. He'd slumped back in his chair as if he, too, was exhausted.

He'd been with her every step of the way. He'd saved her life and her daughter's life and he'd been...here.

'Josh, thank you,' she whispered. 'Oh, love, thank you.'

The *love* slipped out before she could stop it but she was blinking back tears and she had no room to care. Her daughter. *Her daughter!*

'She's perfect,' one of the midwives breathed. 'And red hair, just like her mum. A proper little Irish lass for you to love and cherish. Oh, well done, both of you.' And she'd included Josh because for now he was her partner and no midwife would begrudge him that title.

'All Hannah,' Josh managed, gruffly. 'All awesome Hannah.' And he put his head down in his hands and held it perfectly still.

'Don't you dare faint on us now,' the midwife said, but she was smiling. At some time during the hard, fast labour they'd learned he was a doctor and there'd been teasing. 'It's always the strong ones who go down.'

'I won't faint,' he said, and he lifted his head and met Hannah's eyes and smiled. 'You're brilliant, Hannah. Your daughter's brilliant. Two tough, gorgeous women ready to face the world.'

She smiled back at him, mistily, her hands cradling her baby, her world expanding by the moment. She'd done it.

They'd done it.

'Does she have a name yet?' the midwife asked. 'Or will you need time to get to know her before deciding?'

'I've decided,' Hannah said, smiling and smiling. Life was good. Life was great. Josh was right, she and her daughter could face anything.

'Her name's Erin, after my grandmother,' she said. 'Erin is strong and brave and I love her very much. Both my Erins. And if it's okay with Josh…' She smiled at him, almost shyly. 'I'd like her second name to be Alice, because if it wasn't for Alice you wouldn't have been on that island and Erin and I would be…be dead. Because of Alice, Erin is here and safe. And I love the name. Is that okay with you, Josh?'

Was it okay?

Surgeon bursts into tears in patient's bedroom? Not quite. He managed to nod, to stoop and kiss her—and then he staggered out into the corridor and let it all out.

It was just as well this wasn't his research hospital. Here no one knew him. He was just another visitor.

Why did he feel so much more?

CHAPTER FOURTEEN

SHE'D ASKED ENOUGH of him. Josh needed to be back on the island—there was still mess for him to sort there—but when he demanded who else would look after Maisie and her pups she simply caved in.

How could she not? She had no one else.

She needed to be back in Ireland—she ached for the support the community would have given her. But her father was still abusive, domineering.

She rang and left a message telling her parents they had a granddaughter. No one picked up. She knew they had caller recognition on their phone. It was useless trying to ring further.

She rang her grandmother, who sounded weak and frail, but here at least was a loving reception for her news. Gran wept and told her she was lovely and brave and she loved her, and please could she send a picture of her namesake and she'd hide it under her pillow if her father visited.

'If?' Hannah queried, and there'd been a long silence.

'He and your mother don't come so much,' her grandmother admitted at last. 'Not since I told your father he was a bigoted bully for the way he's treating you. Well, I've told him often enough in the past but I might have got really angry this time.'

'Oh, Gran…'

'It's what he is,' the old lady said resolutely, and then broke off as a fit of coughing consumed her. She couldn't speak again, and finally Hannah disconnected and rang the nursing staff.

'Please… I'm her granddaughter in Australia. Could you check with her for permission and then let me know if there are any changes in her health?'

'She's definitely slipping,' the nurse warned her. 'If you want to see her then you need to come soon.'

These were words that made Hannah feel bereft, for how could she come? The impossibility of travel slammed home.

Bridget rang, but it was a faltering, guilt-ridden call. 'I heard your news from Gran. She's so pleased, so touched that you called her Erin. Hannah, I'd love to fly over and see you but…'

But. There were so many *buts*. She thought of the welcome most babies received in the small town she'd been raised in, and she ached for that community for her daughter.

But she held her baby daughter close, and Josh

was in and out of her room, always seeming to be there just when she needed him, and she decided there was nothing to be done but accept Josh's offer of help and worry about tomorrow tomorrow.

Two days after Erin's birth he was there to take her…home? It didn't feel like home—a barren apartment that she'd left in a pile of boxes and chaos—but it'd be her home and her life from now on.

They walked the block and a half from the hospital—the advantage of living in a hospital apartment. Josh carried Hannah's holdall and Erin's carry cot. Hannah walked beside him, cradling Erin. She felt sun on her face, a gentle wind, the strangeness of being outside hospital with a new little life. She felt…weird.

Josh opened her front door for her and she felt a whole lot more weird.

She'd left a barren, utilitarian, chaos-filled space. Now…

The little kitchen was brightly welcoming, with benches clear of clutter, her mass of boxes gone. A shiny yellow kettle sat on the hob, a bunch of white daisies on the counter. Grimy windows had been cleaned to let sunlight stream in. Curtains now replaced her appalling venetians, fresh, new, yellow and white stripes. Gorgeous.

Giving Josh a look of wonder, holding her precious bundle close, she ventured further.

Into the living room.

What little furniture she'd had had been cheap and nasty, bought or scrounged by herself and Ryan when they'd thought they'd be here for not much more than a year. There was nothing cheap or nasty in what was here now.

Her horrid sofa was gone. The lounge was dominated by a club settee and two matching armchairs, old-fashioned floral, the kind that hid all sins, the kind that said, Sink into me, this is where you belong. Piles of cushions beckoned even more.

'I can even sleep on it,' Josh said proudly. 'It's long enough and there's not a single piercing spring.'

'Oh, Josh…'

'Look at the rest,' he told her.

The rest…

A woollen mat, deep pinks and soft lavender, covered the previously barren floor. A big television was wall-mounted—what had happened to her tiny squint-to-see-it model?

There were wall lamps, a coffee table with a few enticing books scattered on it, and on the wall was a print of a watercolour, the *Cliffs of Moher*, wild and beautiful, a painting that spoke of home but yet was so beautiful in its own right that it didn't cause pain.

'This wasn't all my work,' Josh admitted as

she gazed about her in wonder. 'I rang Madison. She sent me a plan.'

'You rang your sister—about me?'

'I said I had a patient who needed cheering up.'

A patient... Right. Madison would know he hadn't treated a patient personally for years. What would Josh's sister be thinking?

But Josh was opening the bedroom door. What else?

What else took her breath away. Her bed had been miraculously rebuilt—or was it a new bed? Beautiful new bedding.

The serviceable bassinet she'd bought from a charity shop and scrubbed until most of its paint was gone had been replaced. In its place was a vision in pink, a pile of cuddly toys on the stand beside it, a change table, a mobile of teddy bears, a wombat nightlight...

'Madison didn't help me here,' Josh said proudly. 'This is all my own work. Plus a little assistance from the lady in the shop down the road. You'll be thrilled to know I'm now a gold-class client of Cocoon My Baby. You want to see the pram?'

She could hardly speak but she didn't need to. Josh was opening the laundry door. On the far side of the laundry she saw a gleaming new pram-cum-stroller, one she recognised as being far beyond the realms of anything she might have afforded. But she hardly had time to see, for out of the laundry tumbled the dogs. Dudley and Maisie surged out to wag and lick and wiggle. Inside she saw a big, soft dog bed, with four tiny occupants. There was another bed for Dudley. And the door…

'I talked your landlord into letting me put in a dog door,' Josh said modestly, and Hannah thought of the crusty hospital property manager and thought how much money would have had to change hands before he'd have allowed this. 'Oh, and I've been talking to your neighbour. Ruth loves dogs but has never summoned the courage to own one. We've thus removed two boards from your dividing fence. Her courtyard is bigger than yours so now they have what almost counts as a respectable run. Payment may possibly be first choice of pup but Ruth's great. I wouldn't be the least bit surprised if she's over first thing with a casserole.'

She was speechless.

She had her tiny daughter. She had her dogs. She had a perfect home and it seemed she had a neighbour.

She had Josh.

No. She didn't have Josh. He was gorgeous, kind, caring, but she didn't have him. Oh, but what he'd done for her…

'I'll stay for a couple of days,' Josh said. 'Just to see you settle in.'

'I… There's no need.'

'Do you want me to?' Was it her imagination or did she hear a note of anxiety?

Did he want to stay?

'Of course I want you to,' she managed, and it was too much. She sniffed back a sob and hugged him, or hugged him as much as she could. He hugged back. She and her daughter were enfolded in this man's arms. The dogs wuffled and wagged around her legs and her face was buried in Josh's sweater.

Josh might not be here for ever but he was here now, and here seemed definitely home.

The next few days were chaotic, filled with the fuss of babies and puppies, filled with crazy domesticity. If they'd been true partners it would have been the start of the rest of their lives, but somehow the boundaries they'd both recognised the morning Hannah had gone into labour stayed in place.

The boundaries were unvoiced but they didn't need to be voiced. He lay on the sofa and listened to Hannah coo to Erin during the night feeds and he felt apart. As he'd vowed to be apart. Three days later, with Hannah and her baby as settled as mother and newborn could be, they both knew it was time for him to go.

'You've done so much for me already,' she told him. 'It's time you got back to your own life.'

Sense told him it was the truth.

It had made him feel great that he could help her. That he could make her little apartment into a home. That he could cook for her, that he could care for the dogs, that he could watch dumb television while she nursed her tiny Erin. That while she slept he could take her baby and nurse her himself, giving Hannah much-needed rest.

He'd done it for her, he told himself, and if his heart had twisted as he'd managed to get the tiny newborn bundle to sleep against his chest…well, maybe that was satisfaction in being needed as well.

But if he didn't leave now, would he ever? To make her dependent on him… No.

But he could fill her needs one last time. On that last morning he rose early, made her eggs, toast soldiers and coffee—he'd already discovered her favourite breakfast—and took it in to her.

Erin was asleep. Hannah was looking amazing, in pink PJs with purple sumo cats. Her curls were tangled by sleep, she was surrounded by a sea of pillows and she looked cross.

She was staring down at a contraption that looked like some sort of plastic breast. He saw tubes, plastic bags, a wad of tissues—and a glower from Hannah that would have seen off lesser men than him.

'It's the work of the devil,' she muttered. 'But I will conquer it.'

'Conquer what?' But he'd already figured it out. He set her breakfast on the bedside table and perched on the end of the bed as she abandoned the contraption and tackled her egg with relief.

'Bloody breast pump,' she told him darkly. 'I stick it on and nothing happens. Nothing. Then I take it off and milk flows everywhere. But it's early days yet. Roslyn's coming over later this morning—you remember the midwife who was there for me at the end? She's a lactation specialist and has promised to help.'

He frowned. 'So why do you need a breast pump?'

'For Ron.'

'Ron?'

'Later Ron,' she said, and grimaced. 'Forward planning.'

'You're scared your milk might dry up?'

'Not in a million years,' she said, as she dipped a toast soldier and cast another dark look at the equipment. 'I seem to have more milk than a dairy full of Friesians, and I'm planning to take advantage of it. I'm training my body to think it's feeding twins. Whenever Erin finishes, my plan is to pump what's left over and freeze it. That way, when I go back to work in six weeks the women in the hospital creche will be able to feed her my milk.'

What was there in that to make him seem to freeze himself?

'In six weeks,' he said slowly. 'Hannah, you can't go back that soon.'

'Of course I can. Lots of women do. I have a good job to go back to, I had a lovely normal birth and I have creche arranged onsite.'

'But surely you don't want to.'

'You think I have a choice?' Her eyes flashed anger but then she caught herself. 'Sorry. That was uncalled for. But it's a reality, Josh. I'm a single mum on a limited income, but I'll be fine. You've set me up brilliantly and as soon as I can get this contraption working all will fall into place.'

'I can help you financially. That'd give you space to spend more time with her. Hannah, let me—'

'No.' She said it almost harshly. 'Josh, enough. I've needed you and needed you and needed you, but you need to allow me to regain my dignity, to get on with my own life. We're fine, Erin and me. I won't hang on your sleeve a moment longer.'

'I don't mind.'

'No, but I do.' She took a deep breath. 'I can't allow myself to depend on you any more, Josh. You don't want that and neither do I.'

He didn't want to be needed?

He didn't. He'd made that vow three years ago. Almost unconsciously his fingers moved to the scar running down the side of his face. He thought of the first time he'd felt it—as a dressing. His hand had gone to the dressing almost before he'd opened his eyes. Then he'd woken and Madison was there, and the pain he'd seen in her eyes had been bone deep.

He looked down at Hannah, who was consciously focusing on her toast fingers. He looked at the tiny bundle in the bassinet beside her.

How could he let her continue to need him? He'd hurt her. Eventually he must.

'It's okay,' Hannah said gently into the stillness. 'I get it, Josh. You need to be alone. For what you've done... Josh, I'll love you for ever, but now it's time for you to go.'

It was.

Somehow he made it out of the room. Somehow he was packed and he and Dudley were in his truck, and Hannah's apartment was a dreary block of bricks disappearing in the rear-view mirror.

'I'll be back to visit,' he'd told her.

'Of course you will,' she'd said in a voice that had been none too steady. 'There's a little matter of two puppies that are legally yours the moment they're able to leave their mum. Eight weeks?'

'I'll be back before that,' he told her.

She took his hands and she kissed him. Lightly, though, a fleeting kiss, and he hadn't had the courage to take it further.

'A quick visit only,' she said gently. 'Josh, thank you but I no longer need you.'

* * *

His truck disappeared into the distance. She walked back inside and closed the door behind her.

And sank onto the floor and buried her face in her hands.

Why did she want to sob?

'I love him.' She said it out loud and Maisie heard and snuffled out to investigate the pain in her new mistress's voice.

'I'll get over it.' She hugged Maisie hard and Maisie licked her face in canine incomprehension.

She would get over it. He'd been her hero when she'd needed him and that was all. She was now a competent midwife, a caring mother and a responsible dog owner, with no need for Josh at all.

'And even if I do need him…because…

'There's no because,' she said sharply, causing Maisie to back off in confusion. 'Men. Who needs them?'

But Maisie was looking at the door. Dudley was gone, too.

'Oh, for heaven's sake, we need to move on,' she told Maisie. 'We need a snack. Or more than a snack. It's ten in the morning and neither of us have eaten for a whole two hours. We nursing mothers need to maintain our strength. Food's a much more important focus than men we don't need.'

But as she and her dog headed for the kitchen to check the fridge—which was loaded, thanks to Josh's generosity and forethought—Maisie kept glancing back at the door.

As did Hannah.

'They're gone,' she told Maisie, trying to sound sensible, determined, a woman in charge of her world. 'We need to move on. One ham sandwich coming up. Or two? Anything we want, Maisie, girl.'

Anything we want?

She moved into ham-sandwich production but still her eyes kept drifting to the door.

Anything she wanted?

She knew what she wanted, and it wasn't going to happen.

CHAPTER FIFTEEN

THE CALL CAME at seven at night.

None of his research team would ring him at this hour. It'd be Madison, Josh thought, as he abandoned the research paper he'd been wading through and reached for his phone. Four weeks ago he'd resented any interruption, including calls from his bossy big sister. Now he was grateful. It was so hard to keep his focus on his work.

It was so hard to keep his focus on anything but a woman and a baby in Townsville.

'Hi, Madison,' he said into the phone.

'Josh, it's Hannah.'

His breathing seemed to stop.

Why did this woman have this effect on him? Why did his world seem to stop when he heard her?

He'd been to Townsville twice since he'd left her. Well, he'd had to. His team was based at the university, and while he was dropping in it would have been surly not to detour to see how Hannah, baby and dogs were going.

He'd played with the pups, getting bigger and cheekier every day. He'd held Erin, feeling the newborn smell of her, cradling her, being amazed at the changes in her. He'd given Hannah time to wash her hair or duck out to the shops, or do whatever was hard with a newborn baby. He'd stayed when he'd been useful, but when there was no need for him he'd had no place there.

But now this. The phone call. What was wrong? Something was. He could hear it in her voice. He could almost see her, at this time of evening maybe already in her PJs, because that was the most comfortable outfit she owned. Her crazy sumo cat pyjamas? He needed to block that vision.

Why was there panic in her voice?

'What's wrong, Hannah?' And then, because this was Hannah… 'What can I do?'

'Oh, Josh…' She hiccupped on a sob and his world seemed to still.

He thought of Erin as he'd last seen her, a bundle of milky contentment. He'd cradled her while Hannah had taken herself off to get a haircut, and he'd looked into her little face and felt a tug so strong he'd almost panicked.

'I'll come,' he said, and he heard Hannah gasp and then struggle to pull herself together.

'No. I… It's not that urgent. At least… Josh, I don't know how to ask.'

'Then take a deep breath and tell me what's not

that urgent,' he told her, his heart rate settling a little. Nothing appalling, then?

'It's Gran,' she told him, stuttering a little as she got the words out. 'In Dublin. You know I've told you about her. Josh, she's dying. They rang from the hospice this afternoon. She's still conscious but she's fading. The nurses say…well, they can't make guarantees but she's not eating and she's refused a drip. But, Josh, she's asking for me.'

And in her voice… Desolation. Loss.

Love.

'Then you have to go,' he said calmly. 'You'll need money for the fare. No,' he said as she tried to break in. 'It would be my privilege.

'Josh, it's not the money,' she told him. 'I wouldn't ask…after all you've done and I'm not completely destitute. I do have some savings. But, Josh, I can't take Erin.'

He thought that through. Four weeks old… Yeah, there'd be complications.

'We'll have to fast-track a passport,' he told her. 'I know a lawyer in Canberra…'

'I already went down that path,' she told him. 'It's been three hours since the hospice rang and I've been trying every which way since. Josh— Ryan's name's on Erin's birth certificate. In retrospect I shouldn't have put it there, but I thought… I hoped…

'That he'd want some contact?'

'He's her father.' It was a despairing gasp but once again she gathered herself. 'Apparently, I need to get his permission to take Erin out of the country. No exceptions. But I've rung everyone I can think of, his parents, his friends, and no one knows where he is. He's still in Australia, they think, but no one knows for sure and the nursing staff says Gran only has days. Oh, Josh, I need to go.'

'So you need me to care for Erin?'

She gasped again and then fell silent.

'That's what you need, isn't it, Hannah?' He thought of the impossibility of cutting through red tape for Hannah to take her baby back to Dublin. He thought of alternatives. This was the only one, and Hannah had figured it before him.

'There's no one else,' Hannah whispered, sounding almost terrified. 'But, Josh, I can't believe I'm even asking. Of course you'll say no, but this is for Gran, not for me, so I thought... I had to try. I just...'

For Gran, not for me.

Of course not for her. This was Hannah, a woman with a heart as big as the ocean she had to cross to get home. A woman who'd use her scant savings—and by now he'd figured just how scant—to say goodbye to a dying grandmother.

What sort of reception would she get when she reached Dublin?

Cold, he thought. She'd visit her grandmother—

if she was still alive when she got there—but then she'd be faced with a family who'd rejected her out of hand. Would she even be permitted to attend the funeral? Maybe not, he thought, but visiting her gran now, a woman who, despite being close to death, was still of sound mind, was surely an option. Hannah wouldn't be turned away.

He thought suddenly of Alice, of waking and finding she was gone. If he'd had those last few minutes to say goodbye…

'Of course I'll care for Erin,' he said, almost before he knew he was about to say it. 'When can you leave?'

'Josh—'

'Is there a plane tonight? That might even be possible. Our bridge is still down but the weather's calm. I can get a water taxi and hire a car on the other side.' He'd have to pay through the nose to hire a car at this time of night, but some things were imperative. 'I can be with you in two hours.'

'Josh—'

'You'll need to leave me instructions.' He was thinking ahead. 'How much milk have you expressed?'

'I… Maybe enough for a week? Maybe not quite. But I've already tried her on a bottle of formula because I'm supposed to be going back to work in two weeks. She doesn't like it much, but she takes it.' She sounded almost robotic, dazed beyond belief.

'That's great. It means I can augment with formula if I need to. I can ask for help from your midwife friends if I get into trouble.'

'They'll help,' she said, but she said it doubtfully. 'I did think that maybe I could even have her admitted but…'

'But hospitals are full of bugs.'

'And they wouldn't do it. Not for this. If I were ill…'

'You'll be ill if you don't go,' he told her. 'Hannah, let me check flights. Hang on.' He swung back to his computer and did a fast search. 'Yes! There's a flight to Dublin via Brisbane and Dubai, leaving at eleven tonight. I'll see if I can get you on. Flick me your passport details. I can do the rest.'

'Josh…' She was half laughing, half crying. 'You can't just drop everything. Tonight!'

'Hannah.' His voice turned stern. 'You want to say goodbye to your gran?'

Another deep breath. 'I do,' she admitted. 'Almost more than anything.'

'Then we're wasting time. You pack and write instructions. I'll book you on this flight, then call a water taxi and rip Jed away from the telly to organise me a hire car. We're running tight on time, so I suggest you take Erin to the airport with you and we'll do a handover there. Jed can organise me a baby seat so I can take her back to your place and we'll go from there.'

'Oh, Josh…' She was definitely crying now.

'Enough,' he said gruffly. 'Dudley and I will stay in your apartment until you return.' Thank heaven it was a hospital apartment, he thought. How much did he know of newborns? He had enough sense to think he wanted the backup of a midwifery ward if things went pear-shaped. 'I'll need to pack as well. We both have things to do. Go for it, Hannah, let's move.'

'I can't—'

'Of course you can. Right, Hannah. Ready, set, go.'

She reached the airport before he did. The cab driver dropped her off and helped her with her baggage. She carried Erin into the departure hall, tucked herself into a quiet corner, sat on her suitcase and waited.

Fifteen minutes after she arrived, so did Josh.

He strode through the big glass doors and stood for a moment, looking around. He was a big man, dressed in jeans and a black T-shirt, a bit too tight. His leather boots had seen better days. He looked relaxed, his gaze calm and thoughtful. A man facing the prospect of coping with a newborn alone? Not so much.

He looked at ease. Confident. Sure.

In this sea of travellers dressed for travel, coping with the fussiness of checking in, of saying goodbye to loved ones, Josh stood apart.

He'd stand apart anyway, Hannah thought, and then his search located her. Their eyes met and he smiled, and she thought maybe she might cry.

Oh, this man…

'Hey.' He reached her and squatted down to look into her eyes. 'Hey, Hannah.' And he touched her face.

It was a fleeting touch, nothing more, and why it had the capacity to make tears spill…

'I'm sorry,' she managed. 'I can't…'

'You can't think, and why should you?' he told her. 'Sweetheart, you look done in.'

That brought a reaction. 'I do not!' She blinked back treacherous tears. 'I'm fine.'

'Good girl,' he told her, and lifted Erin from her arms. The little girl was wide awake, staring upward at the bright lights with wonder. But as she met Josh's eyes, her tiny face creased.

She smiled.

Her baby's first smile. At such a time…

Josh even had the temerity to produce a man-sized handkerchief and hand it to her. Was there no end to him coming to her rescue?

'Let's get you checked in,' he told her. 'You can have your cry out on the plane, but I'd advise sleep first.'

As if she could sleep on planes… But as he led her toward the check-in counter, instead of heading for the mile-long economy queue, he headed for crimson Priority.

'Josh!' she gasped. 'You can't. I can't!'

'What?'

'Go Business.'

'You're not,' he told her. 'First class or nothing.'

'But I can't pay you back.' This was ridiculous.

'I travel a lot,' he told her. 'By a lot I mean so much that I have points to spare. This is costing me nothing, Hannah.'

'Are you out of your mind?'

'I'm not.' They'd reached the counter and Josh tugged a sheaf of papers from his wallet and handed them over to a bemused clerk. 'We need your passport too, love.'

'Don't call me love!' What was there in that overused word that had her panicked?

'Sorry.' But as she fumbled for her passport he stood watching her with a strange expression on his face. Dammit, she was blushing. Her passport came out of her bag with a rush and fell.

They stooped simultaneously but as her fingers reached the passport, she found she was gripped. Held.

Josh was cradling Erin in the crook of one arm. With his spare hand he held her wrist, compelling them both to stay stooped.

Her eyes met his, calm, grey, thoughtful.

'Hannah, I'm so sorry about your gran,' he said softly, while above their heads the lass on the check-in counter waited with the patience surely reserved for first-class passengers.

'I… It's all right.'

'It's not all right now, but it will be,' he said softly. 'You need to say goodbye to an old lady you love, and then let her go in peace.'

'Oh, Josh…'

'And now you need to gather your strength, go through those big doors and head to the other side of the world,' he said gently. 'And then come back to us. Home is here, and Erin and I will be thinking about you all the time you're away.'

There weren't people behind them—that was a blessing, for Josh's free hand had moved to cradle her cheek, firm, sure. He was propelling her face to his.

One of her hands held her dropped passport. The other was free. She should use it to push him away.

Why would she? How could she?

Came another slight tug, and somehow she was close. So close.

Close enough to be kissed? There seemed no choice.

His mouth met hers, warm, strong, wonderful. His free hand was in her hair and hers in his, so the kiss deepened. Somewhere below there was a baby, cradled between them, cocooned by their kiss.

It felt amazing.

It felt right.

It felt like…home was right here.

'I'm sorry to interrupt, but we're running close to time. We need to get you boarded.' The voice above them was apologetic but firm, and when they broke away and looked up, the girl was beaming a smile a mile wide.

'I do love a romantic goodbye,' she told them, and then she looked back at the papers Josh had handed over. 'I see your return ticket is open ended.' She beamed down at Hannah. 'I'm guessing you'll be back soon.'

'I… That's right.' Josh's hand tugged her to her feet and she felt herself blushing from the toes up. 'Very soon.'

'Well, with this to come home to why wouldn't you?' the girl said, not even trying to conceal a touch of wistfulness. 'Wow,' she said. 'All the way to Dublin and back, and your man and your baby to come home to.' She took Hannah's passport and did a cursory check. 'All's well here,' she told her. 'Gate five, boarding in fifteen minutes. I'm sorry sir,' she told Josh. 'You can't go through to the gates unless you're travelling. But you can kiss her again before she goes through Security.'

'I might have to,' Josh told her—and did.

She sat in her unbelievably luxurious seat, she looked out as the lights of Townsville faded behind her and thought, What have I done?

I've left my baby with Josh.

With a man she hardly knew.

With a man who'd done so much for her already.

She was already feeling sick about leaving Erin. Her arms felt empty. Soon her breasts would begin to ache, but in first-class luxury she should even be able to use her breast pump. She'd have to keep expressing if she wanted to breastfeed once she got home.

Home.

Where was home?

She was going home, wasn't she? To her country, to her family, to the people who'd been with her all her life.

Home was where the heart was.

Home was back with those fading lights. Erin. Maisie. Dudley and a litter of tumbling puppies.

Josh.

'Don't think like that. Don't!' She said it out loud, but in her cocooned luxury there was no one to think she was queer in the head.

He'd kissed her as if he loved her.

Well, that was nonsense. She had herself under control now, or almost. He'd kissed her because she was an emotional mess, because he'd wanted to reassure her, because he felt sorry for her.

Because he was quite simply the kindest, most wonderful guy she'd ever met.

So how could someone like Josh ever want her?

He didn't want her, she told herself, and she knew it was true. He wanted isolation. He wanted no more ties, and didn't she come with ties? She'd just landed him with a four-week old baby to care for. Plus two dogs and four puppies.

She thought of his gorgeous house and mentally compared it with her cramped one-bedroom apartment. He'd go spare. That he was doing this for her…

'How could I have asked it of him?' she demanded, out loud again.

'I had no choice and I gave him no choice.' She gave up on sanity and talked aloud anyway. 'So don't get any dumb ideas, just because he comforted me and kissed me goodbye. I might need him, and he might be everything a great hero needs to be, but I come with baggage up to my ears and he doesn't need baggage.'

'Baggage?' The flight attendant was suddenly right there, with a tray holding water, orange juice and champagne. 'Is there a problem with your baggage, ma'am? Can we help?'

'I… No.' She hauled herself together and thought stuff it and took a champagne—the first alcoholic drink she'd had since she'd learned she was pregnant. 'Yes, I do have a problem with baggage,' she admitted to the woman who was looking as if she really cared. That was also professional, she told herself. This woman was doing what she needed to do, as was Josh.

'I have all sorts of baggage problems,' she told

the attendant, and managed a smile. 'But I can sort them. They're nobody's problems but mine.'

Josh opened the apartment door and carried the tiny, sleeping bundle of Erin inside.

Dudley came in on his heels and headed straight for the laundry door. There was a frantic whine from the other side, Josh opened the door and Maisie launched herself out joyously to greet them.

Followed by four wobbly, wide eyed puppies.

Josh stood in their midst and gazed around him. Hannah had done her best to leave the place presentable, but she'd been rushed and baby paraphernalia was everywhere. The fridge door, bare when shifted in, was now a mass of baby appointment schedules, to-do lists and fuzzy photos taken with her phone and printed on a low-quality printer.

There was a picture of Josh on his last visit, holding Erin, with Maisie looking adoringly up at him.

He was smiling.

He couldn't remember smiling. Didn't Madison say he never smiled?

Two of the pups launched themselves at a clothes horse standing by the window, trying to drag down the edges of a bunny rug. 'No!' Too late. The clothes horse collapsed and baby clothes went everywhere. Plus Hannah's clothes. Knickers, socks, feeding bra…

This felt weird. Far too intimate. Hannah's world was closing in on him.

He thought of Alice and the pain of losing her. He forced himself to keep thinking, biting on the pain like biting on a bad tooth, testing to see how deep the pain went. So deep.

He didn't need this. He didn't want this.

'So why did I kiss her?' He stared down at Dudley like his dog might give him some clue. 'I'm setting up expectations I can't meet. I can't let her keep needing me. I don't want anyone depending on me.'

Why not? Dudley seemed almost to be looking the question.

'Because I have baggage, and baggage hurts.'

And Dudley wagged his tail as if he totally understood, totally sympathised, and then a puppy grabbed his tail and he turned and growled. And then another puppy grabbed his ear. Maisie headed over to nose the pup on the ear away. Then Maisie's nose touched Dudley's and, as if he'd been commanded, Dudley caved in.

He sank to the floor and rolled over. In seconds he had pups all over him. Maisie sank down beside him, Mum having time out, and Josh found himself smiling again.

Erin stirred and woke up, her eyes looking up

at him with wide-eyed interest. Maybe a little anxious?

'Sorry, sweetheart, I'm all you have now,' he told her. We're just going to make the most of it.'

And here it came again, the smile. A smile just like her mother's.

He had baggage?

One baby didn't care.

Dudley had baggage?

His dog had obviously caved in on that as well.

'So I guess my baggage is there to be picked up when your mum stops needing me,' he told Erin, and then he picked up Hannah's wad of 'How to Care for a Baby' notes and stared at its bulk in astonishment.

'Does she think I'm an idiot? I'm a surgeon. If I can operate on a human brain, surely I can change a nappy.'

But…she was wet. And a man could just check.

'Okay, let's get this thing rolling,' he told Erin, and headed for the change table, collecting wipes, disposing bags and fresh nappy on the way. And the instructions. 'Let's just forget all about baggage for however long it takes to get your mum home. Then life can take over.'

CHAPTER SIXTEEN

'*Acushla*… Love…'

Gran's voice was so soft Hannah could hardly hear her. She was fading fast. Hannah had been here for two days and she'd spent almost all her time at the hospice. Gran was clutching her hand, and Hannah was blessing everything that had let her be here. Mostly Josh.

All Josh.

'Show me the pictures again,' Gran whispered, and Hannah complied. She'd managed to connect her phone to the overhead television so Gran could lie in bed and see every image she put up.

She showed the pictures Gran most wanted to see. A baby named for her. Her great-granddaughter.

She had the images on a loop now, so she could talk Gran through them. Erin on the day she was born. Erin's first bath. A selfie where she'd held her baby while a sea of curious puppies took their first look.

Erin being cradled by Josh.

'Stop it there,' Gran whispered, as she always did when it came to this shot. 'Let me see.'

There was a long pause. Gran's breath was raspy, ragged, uneven, but her eyes were alive and wondering. 'Tell me again,' she asked for surely the umpteenth time. 'He's not your babe's father?'

'He's not. You know Ryan left me, Gran, when he knew I was pregnant.'

'Gobshite!' she said, and weak though her voice was, the word echoed with disdain. But then her tone changed. 'But this is Josh. A doctor. He's a lovely man—you can see it just by looking at him. And you'd be the one holding the camera, the one he's smiling at.'

'He is lovely,' she conceded, letting herself drift into that smile.

'And he's waiting for you to come home.'

Home. There was that word again.

Where was it?

'He'll make you safe,' Gran said, gripping her hand with fingers that held far too little strength. 'I know it. I can see it in the way he's looking at you. You'll be loved, my Hannah.'

'Gran—'

'Don't you tell me any different,' she said, hurriedly, with a hint of waspishness. 'I know a happy ending when I see one, and that's what we all need. A happy ending.'

'And a happy beginning?'

'Definitely,' her gran said and gripped her hand harder. 'I wish it, my Hannah. I wish it for you with all my heart.'

'Josh?' The call came at eight in the morning. It was Hannah, and her voice was laced with tears.

'She's gone?'

'A couple of hours ago. I was with her.'

'Your parents?'

'No. They've visited a couple of times but when they knew I was here... Gran insisted I stay so they kept apart.'

'You haven't seen them?'

'Once.' Her voice was stilted. 'Bridget a couple more times, but she's scared Dad'll find out. I'll not be staying for the funeral, Josh. I'm coming home.'

Dammit, what was her family thinking? He wanted to punch someone.

He wanted to give someone a hug.

Instead he moved to practicalities.

'Your ticket is open-ended. I'll book you on the next flight.'

'Thank you. Is Erin okay?'

'She's beautiful,' he told her. 'Turn your video on.'

'Not my end,' she said hurriedly. 'I'm a soggy mess.'

Dammit, he wanted to see her. What was a bit of sogginess?

'So's your daughter,' he told her, managing to keep his voice calm, and he flicked on video mode and positioned his phone so she could see her baby. Erin had been lying in his bed, having her bottle, when Hannah had called. He'd been thinking he should stir and change her—get dressed himself—but he'd been tickling her toes and somehow tickling took precedence.

Yeah, well, he wasn't about to tell Hannah that. She'd think he was totally besotted. Which he wasn't. He was here to do a job. Keeping Erin safe and Hannah reassured.

Only that.

He focused the phone lens on Erin and tickled again. Erin's tiny face creased into her gorgeous smile again and he heard Hannah gasp.

'Oh, Josh. Oh, baby. Oh, she makes me feel…'

'Like you're nearly home,' he said, surely and strongly. 'Two more days, love.'

'Please don't call me that,' she begged. 'It makes me feel more needful than I really am. Josh, after I get home I won't need you any more, I promise. What you've given me is a gift without price. You've been the hero to end all heroes but I won't be needful for the rest of my life. Will you bring Erin to the airport? We can swap over there, and you can go back to your island.'

'Is that what you want?'

'Of course it is,' she said, making her voice firm. 'I won't hang on you any more. I'm strong, Josh, really I am, despite the wimpy-ness you've seen. I can get back to delivering babies and looking after mine, and you can go back to your fantastic research. You know I've read all about it online? It sounds fantastic, what you're trying to do. I found your presentation in Boston on your team's website. The hope you're giving to paralysis patients…'

It needed only this. She was still consumed with loss—he could hear it in her voice—but within her grief she was remembering the hope on the faces of the patients who'd joined the early trials. He and his team were working to attach neural signals to external, robotic skeletons. They were so close…

His work was critical. He needed quiet. He needed isolation.

Did he?

'I need to go,' Hannah said, and he heard aching weariness in her voice. 'I'll catch some sleep now but, yes, please, to booking my flight home. But I promise, Josh, this is the last time I'll ask for help. My need for need is over.'

She disconnected and he lay and stared at the ceiling for a long, long time.

Erin was still soggy, but he was idly tickling her tummy and she was making dumb little cooing noises that signified all was right with her world.

All wasn't right in Josh's world. His head felt like it might explode.

My need for need is over.

She didn't need him any more. That was great, wasn't it?

Of course it was. The vow he'd made, not to let emotional entanglements lead him anywhere that could cause pain, to him or to others, was surely as strong today as it had been when he'd woken up to find his sister had died.

His non-tickling hand ran over the scar on the side of his face. There was his reminder of the chaos emotional entanglement could bring.

But Hannah… He'd kissed her. He'd called her love.

He'd only done that because she'd needed comfort. She'd needed strength and warmth and practical help, and he'd provided it.

He could keep giving it to her. She still needed…

He stopped. His brain seemed to have hit the brakes and was refusing to go any further.

She still needed?

'Be honest,' he told himself, aloud. 'I still need.

'I can't need,' he said, bluntly across Erin's

tiny murmurs. 'I won't put my emotional needs on her. Has history taught me nothing?'

His hand stopped tickling. There was a whimper of protest from beside him and he caught himself. Do what comes next, he told himself. Put emotion aside. Hadn't that been his mantra for years?

So he did what came next. He changed Erin and wrapped her in a fresh bunny rug. He dressed himself and then carried the almost-asleep baby out to the back porch to check on the dogs. It would have been more sensible to put Erin back in her bassinet for a sleep, but he wasn't feeling sensible right now. For some reason he needed to hold her.

The dogs were awake. The puppies had tumbled out of their basket, and the moment he opened the laundry door they were all over him.

He sat on the doorstep and fended them off from investigating Erin, investigating him. They headed down to tumble on the now-worn grass.

Maisie and Dudley flopped down beside him. Obviously after a night spent with pups, adult company was welcome.

This courtyard looked like a bomb had hit it, Josh thought. When the pups left he'd have to spend some time fixing it up, replanting.

Would Hannah let him?

She wouldn't. She didn't need him. She'd said it and he knew she'd meant it.

As he'd meant his oath never to entangle himself again in this thing called love.

When a man takes an oath...he's holding his own self in his own hands. Like water. And if he opens his fingers then he needn't hope to find himself again.

At some time during his interminable convalescence he'd read Robert Bolt's *A Man for All Seasons,* and these words had resonated. For if he let himself love again then surely he'd lose himself entirely. How could he possibly risk it?

Then Dudley jumped up and licked his face, looking hopefully toward the food bowls. Reminding him of the prosaic. The ordinary.

'So I'm being a dramatist,' he told his dog, and took Erin back to her bassinet and fed the dogs and sat down at his computer to check flights from Dublin.

Hannah was coming home.

He needn't hope to find himself again...

He could drift...anywhere.

Or he could find himself with Hannah. And six dogs. And a baby. And complications and domesticity and a laughing, green-eyed girl who'd won his heart.

He needn't hope to find himself again...

He texted her confirmation of her flights, leaving the next day so she'd have time to have her sleep out before she left.

She texted back.

Thanks, Josh. For everything. But let this be an end to it.

An end?

Dudley was now lying at his feet, for some reason looking doleful. As if he knew this time of family was almost over?

Family. There was a word Josh had run a mile from.

He raked his fingers through his hair and headed back outside to look at the pups again. They were a suckling mass of sleepy contentment. Maisie looked up at him and wagged her tail and he thought, She's contented, too.

Dammit, he wanted to share.

Why couldn't he?

Close your eyes and jump.

All it took was courage.

If it was Hannah she'd jump, he thought. Hannah had courage for both of them.

Enough to share?

And all of a sudden he felt…small. Cowardly. Stupid.

And with that feeling, suddenly things cleared. The ice wall was a thing he'd made to defend himself, to defend others, but if all it caused now was hurt… Dammit, surely he could kick it down? Or melt it? Or even climb it and see what was on the other side. Sure, he might fall, but why not try, because the only risk was to be left where he was now. The option made him shudder.

So…kick the thing down? Expose the other side?

'You've got to be kidding,' he said out loud, because that wall had been important for so long. Dudley and Maisie both looked at him in concern.

'I'm not kidding,' he told them, and went to knock on the next-door neighbour's door, because Ruth had offered babysitting and he needed a couple of hours. Now, before he lost his nerve.

Along with everything else, he thought.

But then he thought, What am I talking about? I'll only lose if I don't try.

Or if she doesn't want—

'Don't go there,' he said out loud, because Hannah not needing him was unthinkable.

But then he caught himself and stood for a moment while his thoughts caught up with him. While he acknowledged the truth.

He didn't need Hannah to need him.

He needed Hannah.

The plane landed at dawn.

It was an appalling hour to arrive anywhere, Hannah thought as she collected her baggage and made her way through Customs. She'd told Josh he wasn't to meet her. He'd protested, but she'd been adamant. The airport bus stopped right outside the hospital. She'd meet him at the apartment.

Everything's in order, he'd texted back. You'll find us shipshape and ready to move on.'

Which meant she needed to be ready to move back to the life she'd planned from the moment Ryan had left her. Single mum. Midwife. There was a complication with dogs, but she'd find homes for the pups. And she'd love keeping Maisie.

The thought should cheer her, as should the thought of being reunited with her baby.

It did, sort of, but as she made her way through the gates her legs felt leaden.

Fatigue? Probably. She should have slept on the plane but too much had happened. She was emotionally wired.

She sort of hoped Josh might have disregarded her instructions and come to meet her anyway.

He hadn't. The arrivals hall was a sea of anxious faces but as she tugged her suitcase through the throng there was no one she recognised.

Of course there wasn't. He'd reacted with anger to the thought of swapping Erin over at the airport and of course he was right. To take a sleeping baby out of her cot at this hour… No, he'd be at the apartment, packed, ready to leave.

As was sensible. He knew she didn't need him any more.

So think of practical things. Taxi instead of bus?

It'd cost her a mint, but maybe she could splurge. She was so weary.

But sense prevailed. The bus left every half-hour and it stopped right by the hospital. She tugged her case toward the bus stop…and then stopped.

Stunned.

There seemed to be balloons where the bus should be.

Or maybe they were in front of where the bus should be. She couldn't tell. All she could see were balloons. Rainbow balloons, every colour she could imagine. And in the front of the balloons… Josh.

Holding a baby.

Her baby.

She dropped the handle of her wheelie case and it fell unheeded to the pavement.

Josh was here.

And it wasn't just Josh. What on earth had he set up on the pavement?

He'd brought her a playpen he'd bought when he'd furnished her apartment. 'I won't need that until Erin's at least a year old,' she'd told him, struggling to make him take some of the stuff back, to limit his generosity.

He hadn't listened, though, and it was being used now. He'd set it up on the pavement and tied balloons all around it, helium balloons so they waved and fluttered six to eight feet off the ground.

And the playpen was full of dogs—Maisie and Dudley and four balls of wide-eyed, waggy-tailed fluff: puppies who seemed to have doubled their size since she'd last seen them.

There was a bus behind the balloons. Her bus? People were gathered as if waiting to board but no one was boarding.

They were watching Josh.

Who was watching Hannah.

'I hoped you'd have the sense to catch a taxi,' he told her as she stared. 'But I knew you'd catch the bus. My thrifty Hannah. Welcome home, love.'

And stupidly she said the first thing that came into her mind. 'I'm not your love.'

'That's something we need to discuss.' He walked forward to meet her. Erin was awake in his arms, interested, curious. She gave her mother a huge, toothless beam and Hannah thought any minute now her heart might melt.

Josh eased Erin into her arms, and she stood, gazing down at her baby, taking in every tiny detail, while Josh stood back and looked at them both like a genie might look at Aladdin. Beaming with genial pride. Ready to grant any wish she might make?

Which was nonsense. This was nonsense.

'Why?' she asked, her voice faltering with emotion and fatigue. 'Why have you brought the dogs? And Erin. And all this…stuff. Josh, this is crazy.'

'This is to stop me going crazy,' he told her.

The pups were going nuts. Maisie and Dudley had jumped out of the playpen and were leaping ecstatically around her. The puppies were trying to reach their parents. The bus passengers were looking agog.

'I had to bring them,' Josh said apologetically. 'They're family. I'm sorry about not being in the arrivals hall to meet you but there's some dumb rule about not letting animals past the entry door. So I set this up here. I did give your photo and my phone number to the guy organising the taxi rank in case you decided to be extravagant. If you'd turned up there, we would have done a sprint.'

'With all this stuff?' She was trying hard to make her voice work.

'These people were planning on helping me,' he told her, and grinned at the sea of faces around them—the crowd was swelling by the minute with people were attracted by balloons and puppies. 'This gentleman…' he motioned to a thick-set airport security officer '…thinks he'd like to buy one of your pups. I told him he'd need be thoroughly vetted but so far Maisie and Dudley seem to approve.'

Hannah turned to stare. The guy in the uniform gave her a sheepish wave. 'I like the one with the white eye patch,' he told her. 'She's a ripper. I reckon I could train her to come to work with me.'

'Josh…'

'I know, it's too much to take in,' Josh said apologetically. 'But the thing is, I need to say something and I need to say it now.'

'Need…what?'

'Will you let this guy hold Erin for a minute?' Josh suggested, motioning back to the security officer. 'His name's Michael. He has four kids of his own and he's very reliable.'

But as if on cue Michael's radio alarm sounded. Michael lifted it and listened.

'Yes, we do have a situation down here but it's a minor domestic and it's sorted,' he said into the radio. 'No, I don't need back-up, sir. Yes, we'll clear it as soon as possible but I believe the lady is feeling faint, what with all the excitement. There's a doctor in the crowd. If I give them just a few minutes, sir, I believe we'll have the situation under control with minimum impact.'

He hooked his radio back on his belt and grinned at Josh. 'You heard. Ten minutes. Get on with it, Doctor.'

'Get on with what?' Hannah demanded, wholly bewildered.

'Making the lady not faint,' Josh told her. 'Hannah, try not to faint while I say this because my medical reputation's at stake. Love, I have something to ask.'

'Josh…' She was struggling between laughter and tears. 'This is ridiculous.'

'It is, isn't it?' Josh said. 'And this bus leaves in ten minutes and Michael's superiors might send in the riot squad if we haven't dispersed. No pressure, love, but…'

Pressure? Her lovely steady Josh… Her hero… He'd lost it, she thought. There wasn't an ounce of sense in any of this.

Oh, but he was here, and he was smiling at her.

She was struggling for sense amid chaos. Okay.

Deep breath. She was, after all, a midwife, she told herself. Calming hysterical situations was in her remit. 'We do need to disperse,' she managed. 'Josh, where's your car? We don't need to keep these people here any longer.' Move away, her tone said. Nothing to see here, people.

But it seemed there was.

'We'd kind of like to know the answer,' Michael said. 'He's going to—'

'Don't you dare say it before I do,' Josh interjected. 'Sorry, love, I had to tell them or Michael here would have moved me on.'

'Too right,' Michael said, grinning, and he

reached out and took Erin, and Hannah was so gobsmacked she let her go.

'What…?'

'Okay, this was maybe a dumb idea,' Josh conceded hastily. 'When I thought it through I hadn't factored in Security. But now we're here…'

'Now we're here, what?'

'Will you marry me?'

He said it in a rush, almost panicked, and it brought them both up short. For a moment they stared at each other. Even Josh seemed too stunned to take it any further.

'Help, I didn't get that right,' Josh said, and there were mutters of agreement—and disapproval—from the onlookers. 'Can we try again?'

'Josh—'

'Shush, love,' he told her. 'I will get it right. Give me space.'

'Seven minutes max,' Michael warned, and Josh waved acknowledgement, but his gaze didn't leave Hannah's.

He delved into his pocket and hauled out a tiny crimson box.

He dropped to one knee.

'I can't believe I'm seeing this,' an elderly lady from the bus queue said. 'Ooh, it's giving me palpitations.'

'You can be my fainting lady if I have to explain this away,' Michael said kindly. 'You want to lie down?'

'I want to watch,' she said with asperity.

'Yes, but the bus is due to leave, and she hasn't even answered,' someone else said.

'Bus ain't leaving till she does,' a woman in a bus driver's uniform declared, and Hannah gasped and choked and looked down at Josh.

Who was looking up at her.

Who was holding a ring.

Who was holding her heart.

'Josh, don't...' she said falteringly. 'I can't. You know you don't want me. You're just kind and lovely and caring. You're a hero and you rescued me, but I don't need rescuing any more.' She bit her lip but she made herself say it. 'I don't need you.'

'Don't you, love?' Josh said tenderly, and suddenly their extraordinary backdrop faded into insignificance. Everything faded to insignificance. There was only this moment. This man. Josh.

'You don't want marriage,' she managed, forcing the words out. 'And, honestly, Josh, I don't need it. I don't need you.'

'That's just it,' he told her. 'I've been thinking of all the ways you could need rescuing, racking my brains to think of any way I can be useful. And, honestly, Hannah, I can't think of one. But I'll try. I need to try because... Hannah these last few days... I've figured...my vow to stay isolated was just plain unworkable. Unthinkable. Or maybe it was thinkable until I fell in love.'

'Ooh,' said the lady with palpitations, but Hannah didn't say anything at all.

'You see, there's need and there's need,' Josh said, almost apologetically. 'There's physical need, like hauling you out of sinking cars and delivering babies and—'

'And sex,' some yahoo called out.

'Thanks,' Josh said dryly, but he caught her hands and smiled. 'Yeah, there's sex, and I'll admit that I've pretty much thought of that from the moment I met you. But there's the other need. The need that makes me ask—makes me plead—that you'll become my wife. For I need you, Hannah. When you found me—or when I found you—I was as near to a hermit as made no difference. I might have hauled you out of a car but you hauled me out of so much more. Out of an existence I look back on now with disbelief. When Alice died I pretty much closed down. It took you, my beautiful, funny, strong, wonderful Hannah, to show me how to open up again. To be open to my need as well as yours. To be open to love.'

Whew.

There should be a word bigger than gobsmacked, she thought dazedly. There should be a word to describe—the fact that her heart was about to burst?

'So what about it, Hannah, love?' Josh asked,

and she looked down into his eyes and saw anxiety riding above all else.

He truly thought she wouldn't? It was enough to make her dizzy all over again.

'Two minutes,' Michael warned. 'They'll bring a squad.'

'Shut up,' the palpitating lady snapped, and Michael gave her an apologetic look.

'Sorry, but it won't do a mite of good saying we've got longer. There's other buses wanting to use this bay. So what about it, love?' he demanded of Hannah. 'Marriage or not? Put the man out of his misery?'

And Hannah stared around her at the sea of concerned faces, of these people she'd never met in her life. At her dogs. Her puppies. At her baby in the security guard's arms.

Home, she thought mistily. How could she have thought it was anywhere but right here?

And she dropped to her knees to face Josh.

'What about it, love?' she said, smiling mistily at her beloved. 'Shall we put them out of their misery?

'Hannah… Will you say…?'

'Of course I'll say,' she said, and then she tugged him into her and kissed him gently on the mouth. And then she tugged away.

'And of course I'll marry you,' she told him loudly, as the crowd roared their approval and he gathered himself together and tugged her into what he termed a proper embrace. An embrace that would have lasted…a lifetime?

'Time's up, people,' Michael said warningly.

'No,' Josh said, cupping Hannah's face in his hands and tugging her mouth to join his. 'Time's starting now.'

Baby steps.

That was what Josh had warned her to expect. 'This isn't a miracle, Hannah. There's so far to go. Every step forward seems to produce more complications but this…well, come and see.'

So she sat up the back in a conference hall at one of the most eminent universities in the world, while Josh and his team presented their progress.

Madison sat beside her, clutching her hand. For Josh's sister this was almost as huge as it was for Hannah. 'Of course I'm coming,' she'd said breathlessly when Josh had rung to tell her. 'Josh, I'm family.'

And there was yet more family, for unbelievably Bridget was outside, playing with two-year-old Erin. Erin couldn't be trusted to stay quiet during such an important presentation, but when Hannah had told Bridget she and Josh would be in London her sister gone very quiet. Two days later she'd rung back.

'I'll be there. I'm even telling our father. And I'm coming to Australia to visit,' Bridget had breathed. 'And, Hannah… Our mam… She says she has money Gran left her, and she might just use it to come, too. Can you believe it?'

She couldn't. She'd believe it when it happened.

Baby steps.

Which was what was happening in front of her. The team had left the stage, leaving only Josh and Oscar.

Twenty-year-old Oscar had been a surf fanatic, supremely fit, vibrant, active. A wave had dumped him into a sand bank four years ago and he'd been a quadriplegic ever since.

Three years ago, when he'd had been chosen for this first major trial, Oscar had simply been 'the patient' when Josh talked of him. Josh had carefully made his work impersonal. All the fittings and trials had been done by Josh's team, with Josh working on technicalities in the background. Two years ago, though—post-Hannah— the friendship between the two men had become deep and abiding, and Josh's research had flown because of it.

Alone on the stage, Josh was adjusting the last of the electrodes that wired Oscar to an exoskeleton.

The exoskeleton was a simple brace—or maybe not so simple—supporting Oscar's lanky frame. The first frame they'd built had been so bulky it had been impossible. They now had it down to twelve kilograms—they'd get it lighter—and it took only five minutes to fit.

A simple cap contained electrodes that sent neural signals from Oscar's brain to the exoskeleton. Because of day-to-day electrical interference—such as someone using a cellphone nearby—sensor patches were attached beside Oscar's eyes so he could adjust errant signals with vision.

The five minutes were almost up. Oscar, a big, eager kid, sat in his wheelchair, looking excited.

Josh looked tense. As he should. On this prototype lay hopes of massive international funding, hopes of helping so many.

Done. Oscar grinned up at Josh. Josh managed a tense smile back and stepped away.

Oscar was alone.

He wasn't completely alone, though. In the audience was Josh's team, men and women who'd put their hearts and souls into this research. The entire team seemed to be friends, as Oscar was a friend. They were all now Hannah's friends.

And Josh's friends.

Josh and Hannah's little family now lived right in Townsville. Camel Island would always be their happy place, their place of peace, but it was no place to be part of a community. Their new home, on the hills overlooking the sea, was full of dogs, friends, love and laughter.

And child.

Soon to be children.

Hannah put her hand on her belly and told herself and her unborn baby that they needed to cross their fingers.

Get it right, she pleaded. This was so important.

Josh was standing well back. It was clear to everyone that Oscar was completely unaided. The big kid grinned and let the silence hang. He had a sense of the dramatic did Oscar.

Finally, very slowly, his hand reached out for a glass of water on the tray beside his chair. His fingers grasped the glass. There was a moment's pause as he tested his grip before lifting, then he raised the glass and drank. And put the glass back on the tray.

He grinned again. Then, seemingly almost involuntarily, his hand moved upward.

He scratched the side of his neck.

There were gasps, and then a roar of laughing approval from the audience. This conference was for medical scientists from around the world, doctors and technicians who'd know that to scratch an itch was such a basic human need...

Oscar was laughing with them. Then, with supreme concentration because this was still incredibly hard—there was a way to go with this technology yet—Oscar slowly, slowly rose to his feet. He stood for a moment, steadied, and then took a step forward.

Another. A third.

And then Josh was moving across the stage to

meet him. They stood silent, as if assessing each other, then both raised their right hands.

It was a handshake between friends.

It was a small thing.

It was huge.

The audience erupted but Hannah didn't clap. She'd subsided into her handkerchief.

Her Josh. Her wonderful, magical Josh.

No longer a loner.

A friend for so many.

What was happening on the stage seemed a medical miracle, but it wasn't merely a medical miracle. She emerged from a sob as Josh sought out her face in the crowd, as Josh smiled out at her.

He was her friend. He was her love.

This was their happy-ever-after.

* * * * *